Paul Prescott's Charge

Paul Prescott's Charge

Horatio Alger

PAUL PRESCOTT'S CHARGE

Published in the United States by IndyPublish.com
McLean, Virginia

ISBN 1-4043-2472-0 (hardcover)
ISBN 1-4043-2473-9 (paperback)

TO The Boys WHOSE MEMORY GOES BACK WITH ME

TO THE BOARDING SCHOOL AT POTOWOME
THIS VOLUME IS AFFECTIONATELY DEDICATED BY THE AUTHOR.

PREFACE

"PAUL PRESCOTT'S CHARGE" is presented to the public as the second volume of the Campaign Series. Though wholly unlike the first volume, it is written in furtherance of the same main idea, that every boy's life is a campaign, more or less difficult, in which success depends upon integrity and a steadfast adherence to duty.

How Paul Prescott gained strength by battling with adverse circumstances, and, under all discouragements, kept steadily before him the charge which he received from his dying father, is fully told; and the author will be glad if the record shall prove an incentive and an encouragement to those boys who may have a similar campaign before them.

I.

SQUIRE NEWCOME.

"HANNAH!"

The speaker was a tall, pompous-looking man, whose age appeared to verge close upon fifty. He was sitting bolt upright in a high- backed chair, and looked as if it would be quite impossible to deviate from his position of unbending rigidity.

Squire Benjamin Newcome, as he was called, in the right of his position as Justice of the Peace, Chairman of the Selectmen, and wealthiest resident of Wrenville, was a man of rule and measure. He was measured in his walk, measured in his utterance, and measured in all his transactions. He might be called a dignified machine. He had a very exalted conception of his own position, and the respect which he felt to be his due, not only from his own household, but from all who approached him. If the President of the United States had called upon him, Squire Newcome would very probably have felt that he himself was the party who conferred distinction, and not received it.

Squire Newcome was a widower. His wife, who was as different from himself as could well be conceived, did not live long after marriage. She was chilled to death, as it was thought, by the dignified iceberg of whose establishment she had become a part. She had left, however, a child, who had now grown to be a boy of twelve. This boy was a thorn in the side of his father, who had endeavored in vain to mould him according to his idea of propriety. But Ben was gifted with a spirit of fun, sometimes running into mischief, which was constantly bursting out in new directions, in spite of his father's numerous and rather prosy lectures.

"Han-nah!" again called Squire Newcome, separating the two syllables by a pause of deliberation, and strongly accenting the last syllable,—a habit of his with all proper names.

Hannah was the Irish servant of all work, who was just then engaged in mixing up bread in the room adjoining, which was the kitchen.

Feeling a natural reluctance to appear before her employer with her hands covered with dough, she hastily washed them. All this, however, took time, and before she responded to the first summons, the second "Han-nah!" delivered with a little sharp emphasis, had been uttered.

At length she appeared at the door of the sitting-room.

"Han-nah!" said Squire Newcome, fixing his cold gray eye upon her, "when you hear my voice a calling you, it is your duty to answer the summons IMMEJI-ATELY."

I have endeavored to represent the Squire's pronunciation of the last word.

"So I would have come IMMEJOUSLY," said Hannah, displaying a most reprehensible ignorance, "but me hands were all covered with flour."

"That makes no difference," interrupted the Squire. "Flour is an accidental circumstance."

"What's that?" thought Hannah, opening her eyes in amazement.

"And should not be allowed to interpose an obstacle to an IMMEJIATE answer to my summons."

"Sir," said Hannah, who guessed at the meaning though she did not understand the words, "you wouldn't have me dirty the door- handle with me doughy hands?"

"That could easily be remedied by ablution."

"There ain't any ablution in the house," said the mystified Hannah.

"I mean," Squire Newcome condescended to explain, "the application of water—in short, washing."

"Shure," said Hannah, as light broke in upon her mind, "I never knew that was what they called it before."

"Is Ben-ja-min at home?"

"Yes, sir. He was out playin' in the yard a minute ago. I guess you can see him from the winder."

So saying she stepped forward, and looking out, all at once gave a shrill scream, and rushed from the room, leaving her employer in his bolt-upright attitude gazing after her with as much astonishment as he was capable of.

The cause of her sudden exit was revealed on looking out of the window.

Master Benjamin, or Ben, as he was called everywhere except in his own family, had got possession of the black kitten, and appeared to be submerging her in the hogshead of rainwater.

"O, you wicked, cruel boy, to drown poor Kitty!" exclaimed the indignant Hannah, rushing into the yard and endeavoring to snatch her feline favorite—an attempt which Ben stoutly resisted.

Doubtless the poor kitten would have fared badly between the two, had not the window opened, and the deliberate voice of his father, called out in tones which Ben saw fit to heed.

"What?"

"Come into my presence immejiately, and learn to answer me with more respect."

Ben came in looking half defiant.

His father, whose perpendicularity made him look like a sitting grenadier, commenced the examination thus:—

"I wish you to inform me what you was a doing of when I spoke to you."

It will be observed that the Squire's dignified utterances were sometimes a little at variance with the rule of the best modern grammarians.

"I was trying to prevent Hannah from taking the kitten," said Ben.

"What was you a doing of before Hannah went out?"

"Playing with Kitty."

"Why were you standing near the hogshead, Benjamin?"

"Why," said Ben, ingenuously, "the hogshead happened to be near me—that was all."

"Were you not trying to drown the kitten?"

"O, I wouldn't drown her for anything," said Ben with an injured expression, mentally adding, "short of a three-cent piece."

"Then, to repeat my interrogatory, what was you a doing of with the kitten in the hogshead?"

"I was teaching her to swim," said Ben, looking out of the corner of his eye at his father, to see what impression this explanation made upon him.

"And what advantageous result do you think would be brought about by teaching of the kitten to swim, Benjamin?" persisted his father.

"Advantageous result!" repeated Ben, demurely, pretending not to understand.

"Certingly."

"What does that mean?"

"Do you not study your dictionary at school, Benjamin?"

"Yes, but I don't like it much."

"You are very much in error. You will never learn to employ your tongue with elegance and precision, unless you engage in this beneficial study."

"I can use my tongue well enough, without studying grammar," said Ben. He proceeded to illustrate the truth of this assertion by twisting his tongue about in a comical manner.

"Tongue," exclaimed his father, "is but another name for language I mean your native language."

"Oh!"

Ben was about to leave the room to avoid further questions of an embarrassing nature, when his father interrupted his exit by saying—

"Stay, Benjamin, do not withdraw till I have made all the inquiries which I intend."

The boy unwillingly returned.

"You have not answered my question."

"I've forgotten what it was."

"What good would it do?" asked the Squire, simplifying his speech to reach Ben's comprehension, "what good would it do to teach the kitten to swim?"

"O, I thought," said Ben, hesitating, "that some time or other she might happen to fall into the water, and might not be able to get out unless she knew how."

"I think," said his father with an unusual display of sagacity, "that she will be in much greater hazard of drowning while learning to swim under your direction than by any other chance likely to befall her."

"Shouldn't wonder," was Ben's mental comment, "Pretty cute for you, dad."

Fortunately, Ben did not express his thoughts aloud. They would have implied such an utter lack of respect that the Squire would have been quite overwhelmed by the reflection that his impressive manners had produced no greater effect on one who had so excellent a chance of being impressed by them.

"Benjamin," concluded his father, "I have an errand for you to execute. You may go to Mr. Prescott's and see if he is yet living. I hear that he is a lying on the brink of the grave."

An expression of sadness stole over the usually merry face of Ben, as he started on his errand.

"Poor Paul!" he thought, "what will he do when his father dies? He's such a capital fellow, too. I just wish I had a wagon load of money, I do, and I'd give him half. That's so!"

II.

PAUL PRESCOTT'S HOME.

We will precede Ben on his visit to the house of Mr. Prescott.

It was an old weather-beaten house, of one story, about half a mile distant from 'Squire Newcome's residence. The Prescott family had lived here for five years, or ever since they had removed to Wrenville. Until within a year they had lived comfortably, when two blows came in quick succession. The first was the death of Mrs. Prescott, an excellent woman, whose loss was deeply felt by her husband and son. Soon afterwards Mr. Prescott, a carpenter by trade, while at work upon the roof of a high building, fell off, and not only broke his leg badly, but suffered some internal injury of a still more serious nature. He had not been able to do a stroke of work since. After some months it became evident that he would never recover. A year had now passed. During this time his expenses had swallowed up the small amount which he had succeeded in laying up previous to his sickness. It was clear that at his death there would be nothing left. At thirteen years of age Paul would have to begin the world without a penny.

Mr. Prescott lay upon a bed in a small bedroom adjoining the kitchen. Paul, a thoughtful- looking boy sat beside it, ready to answer his call.

There had been silence for some time, when Mr. Prescott called feebly—

"Paul!"

"I am here, father," said Paul.

"I am almost gone, Paul, I don't think I shall last through the day."

"O, father," said Paul, sorrowfully, "Don't leave me."

"That is the only grief I have in dying—I must leave you to struggle for yourself, Paul. I shall be able to leave you absolutely nothing."

"Don't think of that, father. I am young and strong—I can earn my living in some way."

"I hoped to live long enough to give you an education. I wanted you to have a fairer start in the world than I had."

"Never mind, father," said Paul, soothingly, "Don't be uneasy about me. God will provide for me."

Again there was a silence, broken only by the difficult breathing of the sick man.

He spoke again.

"There is one thing, Paul, that I want to tell you before I die."

Paul drew closer to the bedside.

"It is something which has troubled me as I lay here. I shall feel easier for speaking of it. You remember that we lived at Cedarville before we came here."

"Yes, father."

"About two years before we left there, a promising speculation was brought to my notice. An agent of a Lake Superior mine visited our village and represented the mine in so favorable a light that many of my neighbors bought shares, fully expecting to double their money in a year. Among the rest I was attacked with the fever of speculation. I had always been obliged to work hard for a moderate compensation, and had not been able to do much more than support my family. This it seemed to me, afforded an excellent opportunity of laying up a little something which might render me secure in the event of a sudden attack of sickness. I had but about two hundred dollars, however, and from so scanty an investment I could not, of course, expect a large return; accordingly I went to Squire Conant; you remember him, Paul?"

"Yes, father."

I went to him and asked a loan of five hundred dollars. After some hesitation he agreed to lend it to me. He was fond of his money and not much given to lending, but it so happened that he had invested in the same speculation, and had a high opinion of it, so he felt pretty safe in advancing me the money. Well, this loan gave me seven hundred dollars, with which I purchased seven shares in the Lake Superior Grand Combination Mining Company. For some months afterwards, I felt like a rich man. I carefully put away my certificate of stock, looking upon it as the beginning of a competence. But at the end of six months the bubble burst—the stock proved to be utterly worthless,—Squire Conant lost five thousand dollars. I lost seven hundred, five hundred being borrowed money. The Squire's loss was much larger, but mine was the more serious, since I lost everything and was plunged into debt, while he had at least forty thousand dollars left.

"Two days after the explosion, Squire Conant came into my shop and asked abruptly when I could pay him the amount I had borrowed. I told him that I could not fix a time. I said that I had been overwhelmed by a result so contrary to my anticipations, but I told him I would not rest till I had done something to satisfy his claim. He was always an unreasonable man, and reproached me bitterly for sinking his money in a useless speculation, as if I could foresee how it would end any better than he."

"Have you ever been able to pay back any part of the five hundred dollars, father?"

"I have paid the interest regularly, and a year ago, just before I met with my accident, I had laid up a hundred and fifty dollars which I had intended to pay the Squire, but when my sickness came I felt obliged to retain it to defray our expenses, being cut off from earning anything"

"Then I suppose you have not been able to pay interest for the last year."

"No."

"Have you heard from the Squire lately?"

"Yes, I had a letter only last week. You remember bringing me one postmarked Cedarville?"

"Yes, I wondered at the time who it could be from."

"You will find it on the mantelpiece. I should like to have you get it and read it."

Paul readily found the letter. It was enclosed in a brown envelope, directed in a bold hand to "Mr. John Prescott, Wrenville."

The letter was as follows:—

CEDARVILLE, APRIL 15, 18—,
MR. JOHN PRESCOTT:—

SIR: I have been waiting impatiently to hear something about the five hundred dollars in which sum you are indebted to me, on account of a loan which I was fool enough to make you seven years since. I thought you an honest man, but I have found, to my cost, that I was mistaken. For the last year you have even failed to pay interest as stipulated between us. Your intention is evident. I quite understand that you have made up your mind to defraud me of what is rightfully mine. I don't know how you may regard this, but I consider it as bad as highway robbery. I do not hesitate to say that if you had your deserts you would be in the Penitentiary. Let me advise you, if you wish to avoid further trouble, to make no delay in paying a portion of this debt.
Yours, etc.
EZEKIEL CONANT.

Paul's face flushed with indignation as he read this bitter and cruel letter.

"Does Squire Conant know that you are sick, father?" he inquired.

"Yes, I wrote him about my accident, telling him at the same time that I regretted it in part on account of the interruption which it must occasion in my payments."

"And knowing this, he wrote such a letter as that," said Paul, indignantly, "what a hard, unfeeling wretch he must be!"

"I suppose it is vexatious to him to be kept out of his money."

"But he has plenty more. He would never miss it if he had given it to you outright."

"That is not the way to look at it, Paul. The money is justly his, and it is a great sorrow to me that I must die without paying it."

"Father," said Paul, after a pause, "will it be any relief to you, if I promise to pay it,— that is, if I am ever able?"

Mr. Prescott's face brightened.

"That was what I wanted to ask you, Paul. It will be a comfort to me to feel that there is some hope of the debt being paid at some future day."

"Then don't let it trouble you any longer, father. The debt shall be mine, and I will pay it.

Again a shadow passed over the sick man's face, "Poor boy," he said, "why should I burden your young life with such a load? You will have to struggle hard enough as it is. No, Paul, recall your promise. I don't want to purchase comfort at such a price."

"No, father," said Paul sturdily, "it is too late now. I have made the promise and I mean to stick to it. Besides, it will give me something to live for. I am young— I may have a great many years before me. For thirteen years you have supported me. It is only right that I should make what return I can. I'll keep my promise, father."

"May God help and prosper you, my boy," said Mr. Prescott, solemnly. "You've been a good son; I pray that you may grow up to be a good man. But, my dear, I feel tired. I think I will try to go to sleep."

Paul smoothed the comforter, adjusting it carefully about his father's neck, and going to the door went out in search of some wood to place upon the fire. Their scanty stock of firewood was exhausted, and Paul was obliged to go into the woods near by, to obtain such loose fagots as he might find upon the ground.

He was coming back with his load when his attention was drawn by a whistle. Looking up he discovered Ben Newcome approaching him.

"How are you, Paul?"

"Pretty well, Ben."

"How precious lonesome you must be, mewed up in the house all the time."

"Yes, it is lonesome, but I wouldn't mind that if I thought father would ever get any better."

"How is he this morning?"

"Pretty low; I expect he is asleep. He said he was tired just before I went out."

"I brought over something for you," said Ben, tugging away at his pocket.

Opening a paper he displayed a couple of apple turnovers fried brown.

"I found 'em in the closet," he said.

"Won't Hannah make a precious row when she finds 'em gone?"

"Then I don't know as I ought to take them," said Paul, though, to tell the truth, they looked tempting to him.

"O, nonsense," said Ben; "they don't belong to Hannah. She only likes to scold a little; it does her good."

The two boys sat on the doorstep and talked while Paul ate the turnovers. Ben watched the process with much satisfaction.

"Ain't they prime?" he said.

"First rate," said Paul; 'won't you have one?"

"No," said Ben; "you see I thought while I was about it I might as well take four, so I ate two coming along."

In about fifteen minutes Paul went into the house to look at his father. He was lying very quietly upon the bed. Paul drew near and looked at him more closely. There was something in the expression of his father's face which terrified him.

Ben heard his sudden cry of dismay, and hurriedly entered.

Paul pointed to the bed, and said briefly, "Father's dead!"

Ben, who in spite of his mischievous propensities was gifted with a warm heart, sat down beside Paul, and passing his arm round his neck, gave him that silent sympathy which is always so grateful to the grief-stricken heart.

III.

PAUL'S BRILLIANT PROSPECTS.

Two days later, the funeral of Mr. Prescott took place.

Poor Paul! It seemed to him a dream of inexpressible sorrow. His father and mother both gone, he felt that he was indeed left alone in the world. No thought of the future had yet entered his mind. He was wholly occupied with his present sorrow. Desolate at heart he slipped away from the graveyard after the funeral ceremony was over, and took his way back again to the lonely dwelling which he had called home.

As he was sitting in the corner, plunged in sorrowful thought, there was a scraping heard at the door, and a loud hem!

Looking up, Paul saw entering the cottage the stiff form of Squire Benjamin Newcome, who, as has already been stated, was the owner.

"Paul," said the Squire, with measured deliberation.

"Do you mean me, sir?" asked Paul, vaguely conscious that his name had been called.

"Did I not address you by your baptismal appellation?" demanded the Squire, who thought the boy's question superfluous.

"Paul," pursued Squire Newcome, "have you thought of your future destination?"

"No, sir," said Paul, "I suppose I shall live here."

"That arrangement would not be consistent with propriety. I suppose you are aware that your deceased parent left little or no worldly goods."

"I know he was poor."

"Therefore it has been thought best that you should be placed in charge of a worthy man, who I see is now approaching the house. You will therefore accompany him without resistance. If you obey him and read the Bible regularly, you will— ahem!—you will some time or other see the advantage of it."

With this consolatory remark Squire Newcome wheeled about and strode out of the house.

Immediately afterwards there entered a rough-looking man arrayed in a farmer's blue frock.

"You're to come with me, youngster," said Mr. Nicholas Mudge, for that was his name.

"With you?" said Paul, recoiling instinctively.

In fact there was nothing attractive in the appearance or manners of Mr. Mudge. He had a coarse hard face, while his head was surmounted by a shock of red hair, which to all appearance had suffered little interference from the comb for a time which the observer would scarcely venture to compute. There was such an utter absence of refinement about the man, that Paul, who had been accustomed to the gentle manners of his father, was repelled by the contrast which this man exhibited.

"To be sure you're to go with me," said Mr. Mudge. "You did not calc'late you was a goin' to stay here by yourself, did you? We've got a better place for you than that. But the wagon's waitin' outside, so just be lively and bundle in, and I'll carry you to where you're a goin' to live."

"Where's that?"

"Wal, some folks call it the Poor House, but it ain't any the worse for that, I expect. Anyhow, them as has no money may feel themselves lucky to get so good a home. So jest be a movin', for I can't be a waitin' here all day."

Paul quietly submitted himself to the guidance of Mr. Mudge. He was so occupied with the thought of his sad loss that he did not realize the change that was about to take place in his circumstances.

About half a mile from the village in the bleakest and most desolate part of the town, stood the Poor House. It was a crazy old building of extreme antiquity, which, being no longer considered fit for an ordinary dwelling- house, had been selected as a suitable residence for the town's poor. It was bleak and comfortless to be sure, but on that very account had been purchased at a trifling expense, and that was, of course, a primary consideration. Connected with the house were some dozen acres of rough-looking land, plentifully over- spread with stones, which might have filled with despair the most enterprising agriculturist. However, it had this recommendation at least, that it was quite in character with the buildings upon it, which in addition to the house already described, consisted of a barn of equal antiquity and a pig pen.

This magnificent domain was under the superintendence of Mr. Nicholas Mudge, who in consideration of taking charge of the town paupers had the use of the farm and buildings, rent free, together with a stipulated weekly sum for each of the inmates.

"Well, Paul," said Mr. Mudge, as they approached the house, in a tone which was meant to be encouraging, "this is goin' to be your home. How do you like it?"

Thus addressed, Paul ventured a glance around him.

'I don't know," said he, doubtfully; "it don't look very pleasant."

"Don't look very pleasant!" repeated Mr. Mudge in a tone of mingled amazement and indignation. "Well, there's gratitude for you. After the town has been at the expense of providin' a nice, comfortable home for you, because you haven't got any of your own, you must turn up your nose at it."

"I didn't mean to complain," said Paul, feeling very little interest in the matter.

"Perhaps you expected to live in a marble palace," pursued Mr. Mudge, in an injured tone. "We don't have any marble palaces in this neighborhood, we don't."

Paul disclaimed any such anticipation.

Mr. Mudge deigned to accept Paul's apology, and as they had now reached the door, unceremoniously threw it open, and led the way into a room with floor unpainted, which, to judge from its appearance, was used as a kitchen.

IV.

LIFE IN A NEW PHASE.

Everything was "at sixes and sevens," as the saying is, in the room Mr. Mudge and Paul had just entered. In the midst of the scene was a large stout woman, in a faded calico dress, and sleeves rolled up, working as if her life or the world's destiny depended upon it.

It was evident from the first words of Mr. Mudge that this lady was his helpmeet.

"Well, wife," he said, "I've brought you another boarder. You must try to make him as happy and contented as the rest of 'em are."

From the tone of the speaker, the last words might be understood to be jocular.

Mrs. Mudge, whose style of beauty was not improved by a decided squint, fixed a scrutinizing gaze upon Paul, and he quite naturally returned it.

"Haven't you ever seen anybody before, boy? I guess you'll know me next time."

"Shouldn't wonder if he did," chuckled Mr. Mudge.

"I don't know where on earth we shall put him," remarked the lady. "We're full now."

"Oh, put him anywhere. I suppose you won't be very particular about your accommodations?" said Mr. Mudge turning to Paul.

Paul very innocently answered in the negative, thereby affording Mr. Mudge not a little amusement.

"Well, that's lucky," he said, "because our best front chamber's occupied just now. We'd have got it ready for you if you'd only wrote a week ago to tell us you were coming. You can just stay round here," he said in a different tone as he was about leaving the room, "Mrs. Mudge will maybe want you to do something for her. You can sit down till she calls on you."

It was washing day with Mrs. Mudge, and of course she was extremely busy. The water was to be brought from a well in the yard, and to this office Paul was at once delegated. It was no easy task, the full pails tugging most unmercifully at his arms. However, this was soon over, and Mrs. Mudge graciously gave him permission to go into the adjoining room, and make acquaintance with his fellow-boarders.

There were nine of them in all, Paul, the newcomer making the tenth. They were all advanced in years, except one young woman, who was prevented by mental aberration from supporting herself outside the walls of the Institution.

Of all present, Paul's attention was most strongly attracted towards one who appeared more neatly and scrupulously attired than any of the rest.

Aunt Lucy Lee, or plain Aunt Lucy, for in her present abode she had small use for her last name, was a benevolent-looking old lady, who both in dress and manners was distinguished from her companions. She rose from her knitting, and kindly took Paul by the hand. Children are instinctive readers of character, and Paul, after one glance at her benevolent face, seated himself contentedly beside her.

"I suppose," said the old lady, socially, "you've come to live with us. We must do all we can to make you comfortable. Your name is Paul Prescott, I think Mrs. Mudge said."

"Yes, ma'am" answered Paul, watching the rapid movement of the old lady's fingers.

"Mine is Aunt Lucy," she continued, "that is what everybody calls me. So now we know each other, and shall soon be good friends, I hope. I suppose you have hardly been here long enough to tell how you shall like it."

Paul confessed that thus far he did not find it very pleasant.

"No, I dare say not," said Aunt Lucy, "I can't say I think it looks very attractive myself. However, it isn't wholly the fault of Mr. and Mrs. Mudge. They can't afford to do much better, for the town allows them very little."

Aunt Lucy's remarks were here interrupted by the apparition of the worthy land-lady at the door.

"Dinner's ready, folks," said that lady, with little ceremony, "and you must come out quick if you want any, for I'm drove with work, and can't be hindered long."

The summons was obeyed with alacrity, and the company made all haste to the dining-room, or rather the kitchen, for it was here that the meals were eaten.

In the center of the room was set a table without a cloth, a table-cloth being con-sidered a luxury quite superfluous. Upon this were placed several bowls of thin, watery liquid, intended for soup, but which, like city milk, was diluted so as hard-ly to be distinguishable. Beside each bowl was a slice of bread.

Such was the bill of fare.

"Now, folks, the sooner you fall to the better," exclaimed the energetic Mrs. Mudge, who was one of those driving characters, who consider any time spent at the table beyond ten minutes as so much time wasted.

The present company appeared to need no second invitation. Their scanty diet had the positive advantage of giving them a good appetite; otherwise the quality of their food might have daunted them.

Paul took his place beside Aunt Lucy. Mechanically he did as the rest, carrying to his mouth a spoonful of the liquid. But his appetite was not sufficiently accus-tomed to Poor House regime to enable him to relish its standing dish, and he laid down his spoon with a disappointed look.

He next attacked the crust of bread, but found it too dry to be palatable.

"Please, ma'am," said he to Mrs. Mudge, "I should like some butter."

Paul's companions dropped their spoons in astonishment at his daring, and Mrs. Mudge let fall a kettle she was removing from the fire, in sheer amazement.

"What did you ask for?" she inquired, as if to make sure that her ears did not deceive her.

"A little butter," repeated Paul, unconscious of the great presumption of which he had been guilty.

"You want butter, do you?" repeated Mr. Mudge. "Perhaps you'd like a slice of beefsteak and a piece of plum-pudding too, wouldn't you?"

"I should very much," said Paul, resolved to tell the truth, although he now began to perceive the sarcasm in his landlady's tone.

"There isn't anything more you would like, is there?" inquired the lady, with mock politeness.

"No, ma'am," returned Paul after a pause, "I believe not, to-day."

"Very moderate, upon my word," exclaimed Mrs. Mudge, giving vent at length to her pent- up indignation. "You'll be contented with butter and roast beef and plum-pudding! A mighty fine gentleman, to be sure. But you won't get them here, I'll be bound."

"So will I," thought Aunt Lucy.

"If you ain't satisfied with what I give you," pursued Mrs. Mudge, "you'd better go somewhere else. You can put up at some of the great hotels. Butter, forsooth!"

Having thus given expression to her feelings, she left the room, and Paul was left to finish his dinner with the best appetite he could command. He was conscious that he had offended Mrs. Mudge, but the thoughts of his recent great sorrow swallowed up all minor annoyances, so that the words of his estimable landlady were forgotten almost as soon as they were uttered. He felt that he must henceforth look for far different treatment from that to which he had been accustomed during his father's lifetime.

His thoughts were interrupted in a manner somewhat ludicrous, by the crazy girl who sat next to him coolly appropriating to herself his bowl of soup, having already disposed of her own.

"Look," said Aunt Lucy, quickly, calling Paul's attention, "you are losing your dinner."

"Never mind," said Paul, amused in spite of his sadness, "she is quite welcome to it if she likes it; I can't eat it."

So the dinner began and ended. It was very brief and simple, occupying less than ten minutes, and comprising only one course— unless the soup was considered the first course, and the bread the second. Paul left the table as hungry as he came to it. Aunt Lucy's appetite had become accustomed to the Mudge diet, and she wisely ate what was set before her, knowing that there was no hope of anything better.

About an hour after dinner Ben Newcome came to the door of the Poor House and inquired for Paul.

Mrs. Mudge was in one of her crusty moods.

"You can't see him," said she.

"And why not?" said Ben, resolutely.

"Because he's busy."

"You'd better let me see him," said Ben, sturdily.

"I should like to know what's going to happen if I don't," said Mrs. Mudge, with wrathful eyes, and arms akimbo.

"I shall go home and report to my father," said Ben, coolly.

"Who is your father?" asked Mrs. Mudge, for she did not recognize her visitor.

"My father's name is Newcome—Squire Newcome, some call him."

Now it so happened that Squire Newcome was Chairman of the Overseers of the Poor, and in that capacity might remove Mr. Mudge from office if he pleased. Accordingly Mrs. Mudge softened down at once, on learning that Ben was his son.

"Oh," said she, "I didn't know who it was. I thought it might be some idle boy from the village who would only take Paul from his work, but if you have a message from your father——"

This she said to ascertain whether he really had any message or not, but Ben, who had in fact come without his father's knowledge, only bowed, and said, in a patronizing manner, "I accept your apology, Mrs. Mudge. Will you have the goodness to send Paul out?"

"Won't you step in?" asked Mrs. Mudge with unusual politeness.

"No, I believe not."

Paul was accordingly sent out.

He was very glad to meet his schoolmate and playfellow, Ben, who by his gayety, spiced though it was with roguery, had made himself a general favorite in school.

"I say, Paul," said Ben, "I'm sorry to find you in such a place."

"It isn't very pleasant," said Paul, rather soberly.

"And that woman—Mrs. Mudge—she looks as if she might be a regular spitfire, isn't she?"

"Rather so."

"I only wish the old gentleman—meaning of course, the Squire—would take you to live with me. I want a fellow to play with. But I say, Paul, go and get your hat, and we'll go out for a walk."

"I don't know what Mrs. Mudge will say," said Paul, who had just come from turning the handle of a churn.

"Just call Mrs. Mudge, and I'll manage it."

Mrs. Mudge being summoned, made her appearance at the door.

"I presume, ma'am," said Ben, confidently, "you will have no objection to Paul's taking a walk with me while I deliver the message I am entrusted with."

"Certainly," said Mrs. Mudge, rather unwillingly, but not venturing to refuse.

"It takes me to come it over the old lady," said Ben, when they were out of hearing.

"Now, we'll go a fishing."

V.

A CRISIS.

Before sunrise the next morning Paul was awakened by a rude shake from Mr. Mudge, with an intimation that he had better get up, as there was plenty of work before him.

By the light of the lantern, for as yet it was too dark to dispense with it, Paul dressed himself. Awakened from a sound sleep, he hardly had time to collect his thoughts, and it was with a look of bewilderment that he surveyed the scene about him. As Mrs. Mudge had said, they were pretty full already, and accordingly a rude pallet had been spread for him in the attic, of which, with the exception of nocturnal marauders, he was the only occupant. Paul had not, to be sure, been used to very superior accommodations, and if the bed had not been quite so hard, he would have got along very well. As it was he was separated from slats only by a thin straw bed which did not improve matters much. It was therefore with a sense of weariness which slumber had not dissipated, that Paul arose at the summons of Mr. Mudge.

When he reached the kitchen, he found that gentleman waiting for him.

"Do you know how to milk?" was his first salutation.

"I never learned," said Paul.

"Then you'll have to, in double-quick time," was the reply, "for I don't relish getting up so early, and you can take it off my hands."

The two proceeded to the barn, where Paul received his first lesson in this important branch of education.

Mr. Mudge kept five cows. One might have thought he could have afforded a moderate supply of milk to his boarders, but all, with the exception of a single quart, was sold to the milkman who passed the door every morning.

After breakfast, which was on the same economical plan with the dinner of the day previous, Paul was set to work planting potatoes, at which he was kept steadily employed till the dinner-hour.

Poor Paul! his back ached dreadfully, for he had never before done any harder work than trifling services for his father. But the inexorable Mr. Mudge was in sight, and however much he wished, he did not dare to lay aside his hoe even for a moment.

Twelve o'clock found him standing beside the dinner-table. He ate more heartily than before, for his forenoon's labor made even poorhouse fare palatable.

Mrs. Mudge observed the change, and remarked in a satisfied tone. "Well, my fine gentleman, I see you are coming to your appetite. I thought you wouldn't hold out long."

Paul, who had worn off something of his diffidence, could not help feeling indignant at this speech; unaccustomed to be addressed in this way, the taunt jarred upon his feelings, but he only bit his lip and preserved silence.

Aunt Lucy, too, who had come to feel a strong interest in Paul, despite her natural mildness, could not resist the temptation of saying with some warmth, "what's the use of persecuting the child? He has sorrows enough of his own without your adding to them."

Mrs. Mudge was not a little incensed at this remonstrance.

"I should like to know, ma'am, who requested you to put in your oar!" she said with arms akimbo. "Anybody wouldn't think from your lofty airs that you lived in the poorhouse;

I'll thank you to mind your own business in the future, and not meddle with what don't concern you."

Aunt Lucy was wise enough to abstain from provoking further the wrath of her amiable landlady, and continued to eat her soup in silence. But Mrs. Mudge neer forgot this interference, nor the cause of it, and henceforth with the malignity of a narrow-minded and spiteful woman, did what she could to make Paul uncomfortable. Her fertile ingenuity always found some new taunt, or some new reproach, to assail him with. But Paul, though at first he felt indignant, learned at last to treat them as they deserved, with silent disdain. Assured of the sympathy of those around him, he did not allow his appetite to be spoiled by any remark which Mrs. Mudge might offer.

This, of course, only provoked her the more, and she strove to have his daily tasks increased, in the amiable hope that his "proud spirit" might be tamed thereby.

Mr. Mudge, who was somewhat under petticoat government, readily acceded to his wife's wishes, and henceforth Paul's strength was taxed to its utmost limit. He was required to be up with the first gray tint of dawn and attend to the cattle. From this time until night, except the brief time devoted to his meals, he was incessantly occupied. Aunt Lucy's society, his chief comfort, was thus taken from him; since, in order to rise early, he was obliged to go to bed as soon as possible after day's work was finished.

The effects of such incessant labor without a sufficient supply of nourishing food, may easily be imagined. The dry bread and meagre soup which constituted the chief articles of diet in Mrs. Mudge's economical household, had but one recommendation,—they were effectual preventives of gluttony. It was reported that on one occasion a beggar, apparently famishing with hunger, not knowing the character of the house, made application at the door for food. In an unusual fit of generosity, Mrs. Mudge furnished him with a slice of bread and a bowl of soup, which, however, proved so farfrom tempting that the beggar, hungry as he was, left them almost untouched.

One day, as Paul was working in the field at a little distance from Mr. Mudge, he became conscious of a peculiar feeling of giddiness which compelled him to cling to the hoe for support,—otherwise he must have fallen.

"No laziness there," exclaimed Mr. Mudge, observing Paul's cessation from labor, "We can't support you in idleness."

But the boy paid no regard to this adminition, and Mr. Mudge, somewhat surprised, advanced toward him to enforce the command.

Even he was startled at the unusual paleness of Paul's face, and inquired in a less peremptory tone, "what's the matter?"

"I feel sick," gasped Paul.

Without another word, Mr. Mudge took Paul up in his arms and carried him into the house.

"What's the matter, now?" asked his wife, meeting him at the door.

"The boy feels a little sick, but I guess he'll get over it by-and by. Haven't you got a little soup that you can give him? I reckon he's faint, and that'll brighten him up."

Paul evidently did not think so, for he motioned away a bowl of the delightful mixture, though it was proffered him by the fair hands of Mrs. Mudge. The lady was somewhat surprised, and said, roughly, "I shouldn't wonder if he was only trying to shirk."

This was too much even for Mr. Mudge; "The boy's sick," said he, "that's plain enough; if he don't get better soon, I must send for the doctor, for work drives, and I can't spare him."

"There's no more danger of his being sick than mine," said Mrs. Mudge, emphatically; "however, if you're fool enough to go for a doctor, that's none of my business. I've heard of feigning sickness before now, to get rid of work. As to his being pale, I've been as pale as that myself sometimes without your troubling yourself very much about me."

"'Twon't be any expense to us," alleged Mr. Mudge, in a tone of justification, for he felt in some awe of his wife's temper, which was none of the mildest when a little roused, "'Twon't be any expense to us; the town has got to pay for it, and as long as it will get him ready for work sooner, we might as well take advantage of it."

This consideration somewhat reconciled Mrs. Mudge to the step proposed, and as Paul, instead of getting better, grew rapidly worse, Mr. Mudge thought it expedient to go immediately for the village physician. Luckily Dr. Townsend was at home, and an hour afterwards found him standing beside the sick boy.

"I don't know but you'll think it rather foolish, our sending for you, doctor," said Mrs. Mudge, "but Mudge would have it that the boy was sick and so he went for you."

"And he did quite right," said Dr. Townsend, noticing the ghastly pallor of Paul's face. "He is a very sick boy, and if I had not been called I would not have answered for the consequences. How do you feel, my boy?" he inquired of Paul.

"I feel very weak, and my head swims," was the reply.

"How and when did this attack come on?" asked the doctor, turning to Mr. Mudge.

"He was taken while hoeing in the field," was the reply.

"Have you kept him at work much there lately?"

"Well, yes, I've been drove by work, and he has worked there all day latterly."

"At what time has he gone to work in the morning?"

"He has got up to milk the cows about five o'clock. I used to do it, but since he has learned, I have indulged myself a little."

"It would have been well for him if he had enjoyed the same privilege. It is my duty to speak plainly. The sickness of this boy lies at your door. He has never been accustomed to hard labor, and yet you have obliged him to rise earlier and work later than most men. No wonder he feels weak. Has he a good appetite?"

"Well, rather middlin'," said Mrs. Mudge, "but it's mainly because he's too dainty to eat what's set before him. Why, only the first day he was here he turned up his nose at the bread and soup we had for dinner."

"Is this a specimen of the soup?" asked Dr. Townsend, taking from the table the bowl which had been proffered to Paul and declined by him.

Without ceremony he raised to his lips a spoonful of the soup and tasted it with a wry face.

"Do you often have this soup on the table?" he asked abruptly.

"We always have it once a day, and sometimes twice," returned Mrs. Mudge.

"And you call the boy dainty because he don't relish such stuff as this?" said the doctor, with an indignation he did not attmpt to conceal. "Why, I wouldn't be hired to take the contents of that bowl. It is as bad as any of my own medicines, and that's saying a good deal. How much nourishment do you suppose such a mixture would afford? And yet with little else to sustain him you have worked this boy like a beast of burden,—worse even, for they at least have abundance of GOOD food."

Mr. and Mrs. Mudge both winced under this plain speaking, but they did not dare to give expression to their anger, for they knew well that Dr. Townsend was an influential man in town, and, by representing the affair in the proper quarter, might render their hold upon their present post a very precarious one. Mr. Mudge therefore contented himself with muttering that he guessed he worked as hard as anybody, and he didn't complain of his fare.

"May I ask you, Mr. Mudge," said the doctor, fixing his penetrating eye full upon him,"whether you confine yourself to the food upon which you have kept this boy?"

"Well," said Mr. Mudge, in some confusion, moving uneasily in his seat,"I can't say but now and then I eat something a little different."

"Do you eat at the same table with the inmates of your house?"

"Well, no," said the embarrassed Mr. Mudge.

"Tell me plainly,—how often do you partake of this soup?"

"I aint your patient," said the man, sullenly, "Why should you want to know what I eat?"

"I have an object in view. Are you afraid to answer?"

"I don't know as there's anything to be afraid of. The fact is, I aint partial to soup; it don't agree with me, and so I don't take it."

"Did you ever consider that this might be the case with others as well as yourself?" inquired the doctor with a glance expressive of his contempt for Mr. Mudge's self-ishness. Without waiting for a reply, Dr. Townsend ordered Paul to be put to bed immediately, after which he would leave some medicine for him to take.

Here was another embarassment for the worthy couple. They hardly knew where to put our hero. It would not do for them to carry him to his pallet in the attic,for they felt sure that this would lead to some more plain speaking on the part of Dr. Townsend. He was accordingly, though with some reluctance, placed in a small bedroom upstairs, which, being more comfortable than those appropriated to the paupers, had been reserved for a son at work in a neighboring town, on his occasional visits home.

"Is there no one in the house who can sit in the chamber and attend to his occasional wants?" asked Dr. Townsend. "He will need to take his medicine at stated periods, and some one will be required to administer it."

"There's Aunt Lucy Lee," said Mrs. Mudge, "she's taken a fancy to the boy, and I reckonshe'll do as well as anybody."

"No one better," returned the doctor, who well knew Aunt Lucy's kindness of disposition, and was satisfied that she would take all possible care of his patient.

So it was arranged that Aunt Lucy should take her place at Paul's bedside as his nurse.

Paul was sick for many days,—not dangerously so, but hard work and scanty fare had weakened him to such a degree that exhausted nature required time to recruit its wasted forces. But he was not unhappy or restless. Hour after hour he would lie patiently, and listen to the clicking of her knitting needles. Though not provided with luxurious food, Dr. Townsend had spoken with so much plainness that Mrs. Mudge felt compelled to modify her treatment, lest, through his influence, she with her husband, might lose their situation. This forced forbearance, however, was far from warming her heart towards its object. Mrs. Mudge was a hard, practical woman, and her heart was so encrusted with worldliness and self-interest that she might as well have been without one.

One day, as Paul lay quietly gazing at Aunt Lucy's benevolent face, and mentally contrasting it with that of Mrs. Mudge, whose shrill voice could be heard form below, he was seized with a sudden desire to learn something of her past history.

"How long have you been here, Aunt Lucy?" he inquired.

She looked up from her knitting, and sighed as she answered, "A long and weary time to look back upon, Paul. I have been here ten years."

"Ten years," repeated Paul, thoughtfully, "and I am thirteen. So you have been here nearly all my lifetime. Has Mr. Mudge been here all that time?"

"Only the last two years. Before that we had Mrs. Perkins."

"Did she treat you any better than Mrs. Mudge?"

"Any better than Mrs. Mudge!" vociferated that lady, who had ascended the stairs without being heard by Aunt Lucy of Paul, and had thus caught the last sentence. "Any better than Mrs. Mudge!" she repeated, thoroughly provoked. "So you've been talking about me, you trollop, have you? I'll come up with you, you may depend upon that. That's to pay for my giving you tea Sunday night, is it? Perhaps you'll get some more. It's pretty well in paupers conspiring together because they aint treated like princes and princesses. Perhaps you'd like to got boarded with Queen Victoria."

The old lady sat very quiet during this tirade. She had been the subject of similar invective before, and knew that it would do no good to oppose Mrs. Mudge in her present excited state.

"I don't wonder you haven't anything to say," said the infuriated dame. "I should think you'd want to hide your face in shame, you trollop."

Paul was not quite so patient as his attendant. Her kindness had produced such an impression on him, that Mrs. Mudge, by her taunts, stirred up his indignation.

"She's no more of a trollop than you are," said he, with spirit.

Mrs. Mudge whirled round at this unexpected attack, and shook her fist menacingly at Paul—

"So, you've put in your oar, you little jackanapes," said she, "If you're well enough to be impudent you're well enough to go to work. You aint a goin' to lie here idle much longer, I can tell you. If you deceive Dr. Townsend, and make him believe you're sick, you can't deceive me. No doubt you feel mighty comfortable, lyin' here with nothing to do, while I'm a slavin' myself to death down stairs, waitin' upon you; (this was a slight exaggeration, as Aunt Lucy took the entire charge of Paul, including the preparation of his food;) but you'd better make the most of it, for you won't lie here much longer. You'll miss not bein' able to talk about me, won't you?"

Mrs. Mudge paused a moment as if expecting an answer to her highly sarcastic question, but Paul felt that no advantage would be gained by saying more.. He was not naturally a quick-tempered buy, and had only been led to this little ebullition by the wanton attack by Mrs. Mudge.

This lady, after standing a moment as if defying the twain to a further contest, went out, slamming the door violently after her.

"You did wrong to provoke her, Paul," said Aunt Lucy, gravely.

"How could I help it?" asked Paul, earnestly. "If she had only abused ME, I should not have cared so much, but when she spoke about you, who have been so kind to me, I could not be silent."

"I thank you, Paul, for your kind feeling," said the old lady, gently, "but we must learn to bear and forbear. The best of us have our faults and failings."

"What are yours, Aunt Lucy?"

"O, a great many."

"Such as what?"

"I am afraid I am sometimes discontented with the station which God has assigned me."

"I don't think you can be very much to blame for that. I should never learn to be contented here if I lived to the age of Methuselah."

Paul lay quite still for an hour or more. During that time he formed a determination which will be announced in the next chapter.

VI.

PAUL'S DETERMINATION

At the close of the last chapter it was stated that Paul had come to a determination.

This was,—TO RUN AWAY.

That he had good reason for this we have already seen.

He was now improving rapidly, and only waited till he was well enough to put his design into execution.

"Aunt Lucy," said he one day, "I've got something to tell you."

The old lady looked up inquiringly.

"It's something I've been thinking of a long time,—at least most of the time since I've been sick. It isn't pleasant for me to stay here, and I've pretty much made up my mind that I sha'n't."

"Where will you go?" asked the old lady, dropping her work in surprise.

"I don't know of any particular place, but I should be better off most anywhere than here."

"But you are so young, Paul."

"God will take care of me, Aunt Lucy,—mother used to tell me that. Besides, here I have no hope of learning anything or improving my condition. Then again, if I stay here, I can never do what father wished me to do."

"What is that, Paul?"

Paul told the story of his father's indebtedness to Squire Conant, and the cruel letter which the Squire had written.

"I mean to pay that debt," he concluded firmly. "I won't let anybody say that my father kept them out of their money. There is no chance here; somewhere else I may find work and money."

"It is a great undertaking for a boy like you, Paul," said Aunt Lucy, thoughtfully. "To whom is the money due?"

"Squire Conant of Cedarville."

Aunt Lucy seemed surprised and agitated by the mention of this name.

"Paul," said she, "Squire Conant is my brother."

"Your brother!" repeated he in great surprise. "Then why does he allow you to live here? He is rich enough to take care of you."

"It is a long story," said the old lady, sadly. "All that you will be interested to know is that I married against the wishes of my family. My husband died and I was left destitute. My brother has never noticed me since."

"It is a great shame," said Paul.

"We won't judge him, Paul. Have you fixed upon any time to go?"

"I shall wait a few days till I get stronger. Can you tell me how far it is to New York?"

"O, a great distance; a hundred miles at least. You can't think of going so far as that?"

"I think it would be the best plan," said Paul. "In a great city like New York there must be a great many things to do which I can't do here. I don't feel strong enough to work on a farm. Besides, I don't like it. O, it must be a fine thing to live in a great city. Then too," pursued Paul, his face lighting up with the hopeful confidence of youth, "I may become rich. If I do, Aunt Lucy, I will build a fine house, and you shall come and live with me."

Aunt Lucy had seen more of life than Paul, and was less sanguine. The thought came to her that her life was already declining while his was but just begun, and in the course of nature, even if his bright dreams should be realized, she could hardly hope to live long enough to see it. But of this she said nothing. She would not for the world have dimmed the brightness of his anticipations by the expression of a single doubt.

"I wish you all success, Paul, and I thank you for wishing me to share in your good fortune. God helps those who help themselves, and he will help you if you only deserve it. I shall miss you very much when you are gone. It will seem more lonely than ever."

"If it were not for you, Aunt Lucy, I should not mind going at all, but I shall be sorry to leave you behind."

"God will care for both of us, my dear boy. I shall hope to hear from you now and then, and if I learn that you are prosperous and happy, I shall be better contented with my own lot. But have you thought of all the labor and weariness that you will have to encounter? It is best to consider well all this, before entering upon such an undertaking."

"I have thought of all that, and if there were any prospect of my being happy here, I might stay for the present. But you know how Mrs. Mudge has treated me, and how she feels towards me now."

"I acknowledge, Paul, that it has proved a hard apprenticeship, and perhaps it might be made yet harder if you should stay longer. You must let me know when you are going, I shall want to bid you good-by."

"No fear that I shall forget that, Aunt Lucy. Next to my mother you have been most kind to me, and I love you for it."

Lightly pressing her lips to Paul's forehead Aunt Lucy left the room to conceal the emotion called forth by his approaching departure. Of all the inmates of the establishment she had felt most closely drawn to the orphan boy, whose loneliness and bereavement had appealed to her woman's heart. This feeling had been strengthened by the care she had been called to bestow upon him in his illness, for it is natural to love those whom we have benefited. But Aunt Lucy was the most unselfish of living creatures, and the idea of dissuading Paul from a course which he felt was right never occurred to her. She determined that she would do what she could to further his plans, now that he had decided to go. Accordingly she commenced knitting him a pair of stockings, knowing that this would prove a useful present. This came near being the means of discovering Paul's plan to Mrs. Mudge The latter, who notwithstanding her numerous duties, managed to see everything that was going on, had her attention directed to Aunt Lucy's work.

"Have you finished the stockings that I set you to knitting for Mr. Mudge?" she asked.

"No," said Aunt Lucy, in some confusion.

"Then whose are those, I should like to know? Somebody of more importance than my husband, I suppose."

"They are for Paul," returned the old lady, in some uneasiness.

"Paul!" repeated Mrs. Mudge, in her haste putting a double quantity of salaeratus into the bread she was mixing; "Paul's are they? And who asked you to knit him a pair, I should like to be informed?"

"No one."

"Then what are you doing it for?"

"I thought he might want them."

"Mighty considerate, I declare. And I shouldn't be at all surprised if you were knitting them with the yarn I gave you for Mr. Mudge's stockings."

"You are mistaken," said Aunt Lucy, shortly.

"Oh, you're putting on your airs, are you? I'll tell you what, Madam, you'd better put those stockings away in double-quick time, and finish my husband's, or I'll throw them into the fire, and Paul Prescott may wait till he goes barefoot before he gets them."

There was no alternative. Aunt Lucy was obliged to obey, at least while her persecutor was in the room. When alone for any length of time she took out Paul's stockings from under her apron, and worked on them till the approaching steps of Mrs. Mudge warned her to desist.

———

Three days passed. The shadows of twilight were already upon the earth. The paupers were collected in the common room appropriated to their use. Aunt Lucy had suspended her work in consequence of the darkness, for in this economical household a lamp was considered a useless piece of extravagance. Paul crept quietly to her side, and whispered in tones audible to her alone, "I AM GOING TO- MORROW."

"To-morrow! so soon?"

"Yes," said Paul, "I am as ready now as I shall ever be. I wanted to tell you, because I thought maybe you might like to know that this is the last evening we shall spend together at present."

"Do you go in the morning?"

"Yes, Aunt Lucy, early in the morning. Mr. Mudge usually calls me at five; I must be gone an hour before that time. I suppose I must bid you good-by to-night."

"Not to-night, Paul; I shall be up in the morning to see you go."

"But if Mrs. Mudge finds it out she will abuse you."

"I am used to that, Paul," said Aunt Lucy, with a sorrowful smile. "I have borne it many times, and I can again. But I can't lie quiet and let you go without one word of parting. You are quite determined to go?"

"Quite, Aunt Lucy. I never could stay here. There is no pleasure in the present, and no hope for the future. I want to see something of life," and Paul's boyish figure dilated with enthusiasm.

"God grant that you do not see too much!" said Aunt Lucy, half to herself.

"Is the world then, so very sad a place?" asked Paul.

"Both joy and sorrow are mingled in the cup of human life," said Aunt Lucy, solemnly:

"Which shall preponderate it is partly in our power to determine. He who follows the path of duty steadfastly, cannot be wholly miserable, whatever misfortunes may come upon him. He will be sustained by the conviction that his own errors have not brought them upon him."

"I will try to do right," said Paul, placing his hand in that of his companion, "and if ever I am tempted to do wrong, I will think of you and of my mother, and that thought shall restrain me."

"It's time to go bed, folks," proclaimed Mrs Mudge, appearing at the door. "I can't have you sitting up all night, as I've no doubt you'd like to do." It was only eight o'clock, but no one thought of interposing an objection. The word of Mrs. Mudge was law in her household, as even her husband was sometimes made aware.

All quietly rose from their seats and repaired to bed. It was an affecting sight to watch the tottering gait of those on whose heads the snows of many winters had drifted heavily, as they meekly obeyed the behest of one whose coarse nature forbade her sympathizing with them in their clouded age, and many infirmities.

"Come," said she, impatient of their slow movements, "move a little quicker, if it's perfectly convenient. Anybody'd think you'd been hard at work all day, as I have. You're about the laziest set I ever had anything to do with. I've got to be up early in the morning, and can't stay here dawdling."

"She's got a sweet temper," said Paul, in a whisper, to Aunt Lucy.

"Hush!" said the old lady. "She may hear you."

"What's that you're whispering about?" said Mrs. Mudge, suspiciously. "Something you're ashamed to have heard, most likely."

Paul thought it best to remain silent.

"To-morrow morning at four!" he whispered to Aunt Lucy, as he pressed her hand in the darkness.

VII.

PAUL BEGINS HIS JOURNEY.

Paul ascended the stairs to his hard pallet for the last time. For the last time! There is sadness in the thought, even when the future which lies before us glows with brighter colors than the past has ever worn. But to Paul, whose future was veiled in uncertainty, and who was about to part with the only friend who felt an interest in his welfare, this thought brought increased sorrow.

He stood before the dirt-begrimed window through which alone the struggling sunbeams found an inlet into the gloomy little attic, and looked wistfully out upon the barren fields that surrounded the poorhouse. Where would he be on the morrow at that time? He did not know. He knew little or nothing of the great world without, yet his resolution did not for an instant falter. If it had, the thought of Mrs. Mudge would have been enough to remove all his hesitation.

He threw himself on his hard bed, and a few minutes brought him that dreamless sleep which comes so easily to the young.

Meanwhile Aunt Lucy, whose thoughts were also occupied with Paul's approaching departure, had taken from the pocket of her OTHER dress—for she had but two—something wrapped in a piece of brown paper. One by one she removed the many folds in which it was enveloped, and came at length to the contents.

It was a coin.

"Paul will need some money, poor boy," said she, softly to herself, "I will give him this. It will never do me any good, and it may be of some service to him."

So saying she looked carefully at the coin in the moonlight.

But what made her start, and utter a half exclamation?

Instead of the gold eagle, the accumulation of many years, which she had been saving for some extraordinary occasion like the presents she held in her hand—a copper cent.

"I have been robbed," she exclaimed indignantly in the suddenness of her surprise.

"What's the matter now?" inquired Mrs Mudge, appearing at the door, "Why are you not in bed, Aunt Lucy Lee? How dare you disobey my orders?"

"I have been robbed," exclaimed the old lady in unwonted excitement.

"Of what, pray?" asked Mrs. Mudge, with a sneer.

"I had a gold eagle wrapped up in that paper," returned Aunt Lucy, pointing to the fragments on the floor, "and now, to-night, when I come to open it, I find but this cent."

"A likely story," retorted Mrs. Mudge, "very likely, indeed, that a common pauper should have a gold eagle. If you found a cent in the paper, most likely that's what you put there. You're growing old and forgetful, so don't get foolish and flighty. You'd better go to bed."

"But I did have the gold, and it's been stolen," persisted Aunt Lucy, whose disappointment was the greater because she intended the money for Paul.

"Again!" exclaimed Mrs. Mudge. "Will you never have done with this folly? Even if you did have the gold, which I don't for an instant believe, you couldn't keep it. A pauper has no right to hold property."

"Then why did the one who stole the little I had leave me this?" said the old lady, scornfully, holding up the cent which had been substituted for the gold.

"How should I know?" exclaimed Mrs. Mudge, wrathfully. "You talk as if you thought I had taken your trumpery money."

"So you did!" chimed in an unexpected voice, which made Mrs. Mudge start nervously.

It was the young woman already mentioned, who was bereft of reason, but who at times, as often happens in such cases, seemed gifted with preternatural acuteness.

"So you did. I saw you, I did; I saw you creep up when you thought nobody was looking, and search her pocket. You opened that paper and took out the bright yellow piece, and put in another. You didn't think I was looking at you, ha! ha! How I laughed as I stood behind the door and saw you tremble for fear some one would catch you thieving. You didn't think of me, dear, did you?"

And the wild creature burst into an unmeaning laugh.

Mrs. Mudge stood for a moment mute, overwhelmed by this sudden revelation. But for the darkness, Aunt Lucy could have seen the sudden flush which overspread her face with the crimson hue of detected guilt. But this was only for a moment. It was quickly succeeded by a feeling of intense anger towards the unhappy creature who had been the means of exposing her.

"I'll teach you to slander your betters, you crazy fool," she exclaimed, in a voice almost inarticulate with passion, as she seized her rudely by the arm, and dragged her violently from the room.

She returned immediately.

"I suppose," said she, abruptly, confronting Aunt Lucy, "that you are fool enough to believe her ravings?"

"I bring no accusation," said the old lady, calmly, "If your conscience acquits you, it is not for me to accuse you."

"But what do you think?" persisted Mrs. Mudge, whose consciousness of guilt did not leave her quite at ease.

"I cannot read the heart," said Aunt Lucy, composedly. "I can only say, that, pauper as I am, I would not exchange places with the one who has done this deed."

"Do you mean me?" demanded Mrs. Mudge.

"You can tell best."

"I tell you what, Aunt Lucy Lee," said Mrs. Mudge, her eyes blazing with anger, "If you dare insinuate to any living soul that I stole your paltry money, which I don't believe you ever had, I will be bitterly revenged upon you."

She flaunted out of the room, and Aunt Lucy, the first bitterness of her disappointment over, retired to bed, and slept more tranquilly than the unscrupulous woman who had robbed her.

At a quarter before four Paul started from his humble couch, and hastily dressed himself, took up a little bundle containing all his scanty stock of clothing, and noiselessly descended the two flights of stairs which separated him from the lower story. Here he paused a moment for Aunt Lucy to appear. Her sharp ears had distinguished his stealthy steps as he passed her door, and she came down to bid him good-by. She had in her hands a pair of stockings which she slipped into his bundle.

"I wish I had something else to give you, Paul," she said, "but you know that I am not very rich."

"Dear Aunt Lucy," said Paul, kissing her, "you are my only friend on earth. You have been very kind to me, and I never will forget you, NEVER! By-and-by, when I am rich, I will build a fine house, and you will come and live with me, won't you?"

Paul's bright anticipations, improbable as they were, had the effect of turning his companion's thoughts into a more cheerful channel.

She bent down and kissed him, whispering softly, "Yes, I will, Paul."

"Then it's a bargain," said he, joyously, "Mind you don't forget it. I shall come for you one of these days when you least expect it."

"Have you any money?" inquired Aunt Lucy.

Paul shook his head.

"Then," said she, drawing from her finger a gold ring which had held its place for many long years, "here is something which will bring you a little money if you are ever in distress."

Paul hung back.

"I would rather not take it, indeed I would," he said, earnestly, "I would rather go hungry for two or three days than sell your ring. Besides, I shall not need it; God will provide for me."

"But you need not sell it," urged Aunt Lucy, "unless it is absolutely necessary. You can take it and keep it in remembrance of me. Keep it till you see me again, Paul. It will be a pledge to me that you will come back again some day."

"On that condition I will take it," said Paul, "and some day I will bring it back."

A slight noise above, as of some one stirring in sleep, excited the apprehensions of the two, and warned them that it was imprudent for them to remain longer in conversation.

After a hurried good-by, Aunt Lucy quietly went upstairs again, and Paul, shouldering his bundle, walked rapidly away.

The birds, awakening from their night's repose, were beginning to carol forth their rich songs of thanksgiving for the blessing of a new day. From the flowers beneath his feet and the blossom-laden branches above his head, a delicious perfume floated out upon the morning air, and filled the heart of the young wanderer with a sense of the joyousness of existence, and inspired him with a hopeful confidence in the future.

For the first time he felt that he belonged to himself. At the age of thirteen he had taken his fortune in his own hand, and was about to mold it as best he might.

There were care, and toil, and privations before him, no doubt, but in that bright morning hour he could harbor only cheerful and trusting thoughts. Hopefully he looked forward to the time when he could fulfil his father's dying injunction, and lift from his name the burden of a debt unpaid. Then his mind reverting to another thought, he could not help smiling at the surprise and anger of Mr. Mudge, when he should find that his assistant had taken French leave. He thought he should like to be concealed somewhere where he could witness the commotion excited by his own departure. But as he could not be in two places at the same time, he must lose that satisfaction. He had cut loose from the Mudge household, as he trusted, forever. He felt that a new and brighter life was opening before him.

VIII.

A FRIEND IN NEED.

Our hero did not stop till he had put a good five miles between himself and the poorhouse. He knew that it would not be long before Mr. Mudge would discover his absence, and the thought of being carried back was doubly distasteful to him now that he had, even for a short time, felt the joy of being his own master. His hurried walk, taken in the fresh morning air, gave him quite a sharp appetite. Luckily he had the means of gratifying it. The night before he had secreted half his supper, knowing that he should need it more the next morning. He thought he might now venture to sit down and eat it.

At a little distance from the road was a spring, doubtless used for cattle, since it was situated at the lower end of a pasture. Close beside and bending over it was a broad, branching oak, which promised a cool and comfortable shelter.

"That's just the place for me," thought Paul, who felt thirsty as well as hungry, "I think I will take breakfast here and rest awhile before I go any farther."

So saying he leaped lightly over the rail fence, and making his way to the place indicated, sat down in the shadow of the tree. Scooping up some water in the hollow of his hand, he drank a deep and refreshing draught. He next proceeded to pull out of his pocket a small package, which proved to contain two small pieces of bread. His long morning walk had given him such an appetite that he was not long in despatching all he had. It is said by some learned physicians, who no doubt understand the matter, that we should always rise from the table with an appetite. Probably Paul had never heard of this rule. Nevertheless, he seemed in a fair way of putting it into practice, for the best of reasons, because he could not help it.

His breakfast, though not the most inviting, being simply unbuttered bread and rather dry at that, seemed more delicious than ever before, but unfortunately there was not enough of it. However, as there seemed likely to be no more forth-coming, he concluded in default of breakfast to lie down under the tree for a few minutes before resuming his walk. Though he could not help wondering vague-ly where his dinner was to come from, as that time was several hours distant, he wisely decided not to anticipate trouble till it came.

Lying down under the tree, Paul began to consider what Mr. Mudge would say when he discovered that he had run away.

"He'll have to milk the cows himself," thought Paul. "He won't fancy that much. Won't Mrs. Mudge scold, thought? I'm glad I shan't be within hearing."

"Holloa!"

It was a boy's voice that Paul heard.

Looking up he saw a sedate company of cows entering the pasture single file through an aperture made by letting down the bars. Behind them walked a boy of about his own size, flourishing a stout hickory stick. The cows went directly to the spring from which Paul had already drunk. The young driver looked at our hero with some curiosity, wondering, doubtless, what brought him there so early in the morning. After a little hesitation he said, remarking Paul's bundle, "Where are you traveling?"

"I don't know exactly," said Paul, who was not quite sure whether it would be politic to avow his destination.

"Don't know?" returned the other, evidently surprised.

"Not exactly; I may go to New York."

"New York! That's a great ways off. Do you know the way there?"

"No, but I can find it."

"Are you going all alone?" asked his new acquaintance, who evidently thought Paul had undertaken a very formidable journey.

"Yes."

"Are you going to walk all the way?"

"Yes, unless somebody offers me a ride now and then."

"But why don't you ride in the stage, or in the cars? You would get there a good deal quicker."

"One reason," said Paul, hesitating a little, "is because I have no money to pay for riding."

"Then how do you expect to live? Have you had any breakfast, this morning?"

"I brought some with me, and just got through eating it when you came along."

"And where do you expect to get any dinner?" pursued his questioner, who was evidently not a little puzzled by the answers he received.

"I don't know," returned Paul.

His companion looked not a little confounded at this view of the matter, but presently a bright thought struck him.

"I shouldn't wonder," he said, shrewdly, "if you were running away."

Paul hesitated a moment. He knew that his case must look a little suspicious, thus unexplained, and after a brief pause for reflection determined to take the questioner into his confidence. He did this the more readily because his new acquaintance looked very pleasant.

"You've guessed right," he said; "if you'll promise not to tell anybody, I'll tell you all about it."

This was readily promised, and the boy who gave his name as John Burgess, sat down beside Paul, while he, with the frankness of boyhood, gave a circumstantial account of his father's death, and the ill-treatment he had met with subsequently.

"Do you come from Wrenville?" asked John, interested. "Why, I've got relations there. Perhaps you know my cousin, Ben Newcome."

"Is Ben Newcome your cousin? O yes, I know him very well; he's a first-rate fellow."

"He isn't much like his father."

"Not at all. If he was"—

"You wouldn't like him so well. Uncle talks a little too much out of the dictionary, and walks so straight that he bends backward. But I say, Paul, old Mudge deserves to be choked, and Mrs. Mudge should be obliged to swallow a gallon of her own soup. I don't know but that would be worse than choking. I wouldn't have stayed so long if I had been in your place."

"I shouldn't," said Paul, "if it hadn't been for Aunt Lucy."

"Was she an aunt of yours?"

"No, but we used to call her so, She's the best friend I've got, and I don't know but the only one," said Paul, a little sadly.

"No, she isn't," said John, quickly; "I'll be your friend, Paul. Sometime, perhaps, I shall go to New York, myself, and then I will come and see you. Where do you expect to be?"

"I don't know anything about the city," said Paul, "but if you come, I shall be sure to see you somewhere. I wish you were going now."

Neither Paul nor his companion had much idea of the extent of the great metropolis, or they would not have taken it so much as a matter of course that, being in the same place, they should meet each other.

Their conversation was interrupted by the ringing of a bell from a farmhouse within sight.

"That's our breakfast-bell," said John rising from the grass. "It is meant for me. I suppose they wonder what keeps me so long. Won't you come and take breakfast with me, Paul?"

"I guess not," said Paul, who would have been glad to do so had he followed the promptings of his appetite. "I'm afraid your folks would ask me questions, and then it would be found out that I am running away."

"I didn't think of that," returned John, after a pause. "You haven't got any dinner with you?" he said a moment after.

"No."

"Well, I'll tell you what I'll do. Come with me as far as the fence, and lie down there till I've finished breakfast. Then I'll bring something out for you, and maybe I'll walk along a little way with you."

"You are very kind," said Paul, gratefully.

"Oh, nonsense," said John, "that's nothing. Besides, you know we are going to be friends."

"John! breakfast's ready."

"There's Nelson calling me," said John, hurriedly. "I must leave you; there's the fence; lie down there, and I'll be back in a jiffy."

"John, I say, why don't you come?"

"I'm coming. You mustn't think everybody's got such a thundering great appetite as you, Nelson."

"I guess you've got enough to keep you from pining away," said Nelson, good-naturedly, "you're twice as fat as I am."

"That's because I work harder," said John, rather illogically.

The brothers went in to breakfast.

But a few minutes elapsed before John reappeared, bearing under his arm a parcel wrapped up in an old newspaper. He came up panting with the haste he had made.

"It didn't take you long to eat breakfast," said Paul.

"No, I hurried through it; I thought you would get tired of waiting. And now I'll walk along with you a little ways. But wait here's something for you."

So saying he unrolled the newspaper and displayed a loaf of bread, fresh and warm, which looked particularly inviting to Paul, whose scanty breakfast had by no means satisfied his appetite. Besides this, there was a loaf of molasses ginger-bread, with which all who were born in the country, or know anything of New England housekeeping, are familiar.

"There," said John, "I guess that'll be enough for your dinner."

"But how did you get it without having any questions asked?" inquired our hero.

"Oh," said John, "I asked mother for them, and when she asked what I wanted of them, I told her that I'd answer that question to-morrow. You see I wanted to give you a chance to get off out of the way, though mother wouldn't tell, even if she knew."

"All right," said Paul, with satisfaction.

He could not help looking wistfully at the bread, which looked very inviting to one accustomed to poorhouse fare.

"If you wouldn't mind," he said hesitating, "I would like to eat a little of the bread now."

"Mind, of course not," said John, breaking off a liberal slice. "Why didn't I think of that before? Walking must have given you a famous appetite."

John looked on with evident approbation, while Paul ate with great apparent appetite.

"There," said he with a sigh of gratification, as he swallowed the last morsel, "I haven't tasted anything so good for a long time."

"Is it as good as Mrs. Mudge's soup?" asked John, mischievously.

"Almost," returned Paul, smiling.

We must now leave the boys to pursue their way, and return to the dwelling from which our hero had so unceremoniously taken his departure, and from which danger now threatened him.

IX.

A CLOUD IN THE MUDGE HORIZON.

Mr. Mudge was accustomed to call Paul at five o'clock, to milk the cows and perform other chores. He himself did not rise till an hour later. During Paul's sickness, he was obliged to take his place,—a thing he did not relish overmuch. Now that our hero had recovered, he gladly prepared to indulge himself in an extra nap.

"Paul!" called Mr. Mudge from the bottom of the staircase leading up into the attic, "it's five o'clock; time you were downstairs."

Mr. Mudge waited for an answer, but none came.

"Paul!" repeated Mr. Mudge in a louder tone, "it's time to get up; tumble out there." Again there was no answer.

At first, Mr. Mudge thought it might be in consequence of Paul's sleeping so soundly, but on listening attentively, he could not distinguish the deep and regular breathing which usually accompanies such slumber.

"He must be sullen," he concluded, with a feeling of irritation. "If he is, I'll teach him——"

Without taking time to finish the sentence, he bounded up the rickety staircase, and turned towards the bed with the intention of giving our hero a smart shaking.

He looked with astonishment at the empty bed. "Is it possible," he thought, "that Paul has already got up? He isn't apt to do so before he is called."

At this juncture, Mrs. Mudge, surprised at her husband's prolonged absence, called from below, "Mr. Mudge!"

"Well, wife?"

"What in the name of wonder keeps you up there so long?"

"Just come up and see."

Mrs. Mudge did come up. Her husband pointed to the empty bed.

"What do you think of that?" he asked.

"What about it?" she inquired, not quite comprehending.

"About that boy, Paul. When I called him I got no answer, so I came up, and behold he is among the missing."

"You don't think he's run away, do you?" asked Mrs. Mudge startled.

"That is more than I know."

"I'll see if his clothes are here," said his wife, now fully aroused.

Her search was unavailing. Paul's clothes had disappeared as mysteriously as their owner.

"It's a clear case," said Mr. Mudge, shaking his head; "he's gone. I wouldn't have lost him for considerable. He was only a boy, but I managed to get as much work out of him as a man. The question is now, what shall we do about it?"

"He must be pursued," said Mrs. Mudge, with vehemence, "I'll have him back if it costs me twenty dollars. I'll tell you what, husband," she exclaimed, with a sudden light breaking in upon her, "if there's anybody in this house knows where he's gone, it is Aunt Lucy Lee. Only last week I caught her knitting him a pair of stockings. I might have known what it meant if I hadn't been a fool."

"Ha, ha! So you might, if you hadn't been a fool!" echoed a mocking voice.

Turning with sudden anger, Mrs. Mudge beheld the face of the crazy girl peering up at her from below.

This turned her thoughts into a different channel.

"I'll teach you what I am," she exclaimed, wrathfully descending the stairs more rapidly than she had mounted them, "and if you know anything about the little scamp, I'll have it out of you."

The girl narrowly succeeded in eluding the grasp of her pursuer. But, alas! for Mrs. Mudge. In her impetuosity she lost her footing, and fell backward into a pail of water which had been brought up the night before and set in the entry for purposes of ablution. More wrathful than ever, Mrs. Mudge bounced into her room and sat down in her dripping garments in a very uncomfortable frame of mind. As for Paul, she felt a personal dislike for him, and was not sorry on some accounts to have him out of the house. The knowledge, however, that he had in a manner defied her authority by running away, filled her with an earnest desire to get him back, if only to prove that it was not to be defied with impunity.

Hoping to elicit some information from Aunt Lucy, who, she felt sure, was in Paul's confidence, she paid her a visit.

"Well, here's a pretty goings on," she commenced, abruptly. Finding that Aunt Lucy manifested no curiosity on the subject, she continued, in a significant tone, "Of course, YOU don't know anything about it."

"I can tell better when I know what you refer to," said the old lady calmly.

"Oh, you are very ignorant all at once. I suppose you didn't know Paul Prescott had run away?"

"I am not surprised," said the old lady, in the same quiet manner.

Mrs. Mudge had expected a show of astonishment, and this calmness disconcerted her.

"You are not surprised!" she retorted. "I presume not, since you knew all about it beforehand. That's why you were knitting him some stockings. Deny it, if you dare."

"I have no disposition to deny it."

"You haven't!" exclaimed the questioner, almost struck dumb with this audacity.

"No," said Aunt Lucy. "Why should I? There was no particular inducement for him to stay here. Wherever he goes, I hope he will meet with good friends and good treatment."

"As much as to say he didn't find them here. Is that what you mean?"

"I have no charges to bring."

"But I have," said Mrs. Mudge, her eyes lighting with malicious satisfaction. "Last night you missed a ten-dollar gold piece, which you saw was stolen from you. This morning it appears that Paul Prescott has run away. I charge him with the theft."

"You do not, can not believe this," said the old lady, uneasily.

"Of course I do," returned Mrs. Mudge, triumphantly, perceiving her advantage. "I have no doubt of it, and when we get the boy back, he shall be made to confess it."

Aunt Lucy looked troubled, much to the gratification of Mrs. Mudge. It was but for a short time, however. Rising from her seat, she stood confronting Mrs. Mudge, and said quietly, but firmly, "I have no doubt, Mrs. Mudge, you are capable of doing what you say. I would advise you, however, to pause. You know, as well as I do, that Paul is incapable of this theft. Even if he were wicked enough to form the idea, he would have no need, since it was my intention to GIVE him this money. Who did actually steal the gold, you PERHAPS know better than I. Should it be necessary, I shall not hesitate to say so. I advise you not to render it necessary."

The threat which lay in these words was understood. It came with the force of a sudden blow to Mrs. Mudge, who had supposed it would be no difficult task to frighten and silence Aunt Lucy. The latter had always been so yielding in all matters relating to herself, that this intrepid championship of Paul's interests was unlooked for. The tables were completely turned. Pale with rage, and a mortified sense of having been foiled with her own weapons, Mrs. Mudge left the room.

Meanwhile her husband milked the cows, and was now occupied in performing certain other duties that could not be postponed, being resolved, immediately after breakfast was over, to harness up and pursue the runaway.

"Well, did you get anything out of the old lady?" he inquired, as he came from the barn with the full milk-pails.

"She said she knew beforehand that he was going."

"Eh!" said Mr. Mudge, pricking up his ears, "did she say where?"

"No, and she won't. She knit him a pair of stockings to help him off, and does-n't pretend to deny it. She's taken a wonderful fancy to the young scamp, and has been as obstinate as could be ever since he has been here."

"If I get him back," said Mr. Mudge, "he shall have a good flogging, if I am able to give him one, and she shall be present to see it."

"That's right," said Mrs. Mudge, approvingly, "when are you going to set out after him?"

"Right after breakfast. So be spry, and get it ready as soon as you can."

Under the stimulus of this inspiring motive, Mrs. Mudge bustled about with new energy, and before many minutes the meal was in readiness. It did not take long to dispatch it. Immediately afterwards, Mr. Mudge harnessed up, as he had deter-mined, and started off in pursuit of our hero.

In the meantime the two boys had walked leisurely along, conversing on various subjects.

"When you get to the city, Paul," said John, "I shall want to hear from you. Will you write to me?"

Paul promised readily.

"You can direct to John Burges, Burrville. The postmaster knows me, and I shall be sure to get it."

"I wish you were going with me," said Paul.

"Sometimes when I think that I am all alone it discourages me. It would be so much pleasanter to have some one with me."

"I shall come sometime," said John, "when I am a little older. I heard father say something the other day about my going into a store in the city. So we may meet again."

"I hope we shall."

They were just turning a bend of the road, when Paul chanced to look backward. About a quarter of a mile back he descried a horse and wagon wearing a familiar look. Fixing his eyes anxiously upon them, he was soon made aware that his suspicions were only too well founded. It was Mr. Mudge, doubtless in quest of him.

"What shall I do?" he asked, hurriedly of his companion.

"What's the matter?"

This was quickly explained.

John was quickwitted, and he instantly decided upon the course proper to be pursued. On either side of the road was a growth of underbrush so thick as to be almost impenetrable.

"Creep in behind there, and be quick about it," directed John, "there is no time to lose."

"There," said he, after Paul had followed his advice, "if he can see you now he must have sharp eyes."

"Won't you come in too?"

"Not I," said John, "I am anxious to see this Mr. Mudge, since you have told me so much about him. I hope he will ask me some questions."

"What will you tell him?"

"Trust me for that. Don't say any more. He's close by."

X.

MR. MUDGE MEETS HIS MATCH.

John lounged along, appearing to be very busily engaged in making a whistle from a slip of willow which he had a short time before cut from the tree. He purposely kept in the middle of the road, apparently quite unaware of the approach of the vehicle, until he was aroused by the sound of a voice behind him.

"Be a little more careful, if you don't want to get run over."

John assumed a look of surprise, and with comic terror ran to the side of the road.

Mr. Mudge checked his horse, and came to a sudden halt.

"I say, youngster, haven't you seen a boy of about your own size walking along, with a bundle in his hand?"

"Tied up in a red cotton handkerchief?" inquired John.

"Yes, I believe so," said Mr. Mudge, eagerly, "where did you———"

"With a blue cloth cap?"

"Yes, where———"

"Gray jacket and pants?"

"Yes, yes. Where?"

"With a patch on one knee?"

"Yes, the very one. When did you see him?" said Mr. Mudge, getting ready to start his horse.

"Perhaps it isn't the one you mean," continued John, who took a mischievous delight in playing with the evident impatience of Mr. Mudge; "the boy that I saw looked thin, as if he hadn't had enough to eat."

Mr. Mudge winced slightly, and looked at John with some suspicion. But John put on so innocent and artless a look that Mr. Mudge at once dismissed the idea that there was any covert meaning in what he said. Meanwhile Paul, from his hiding-place in the bushes, had listened with anxiety to the foregoing colloquy. When John described his appearance so minutely, he was seized with a sudden apprehension that the boy meant to betray him. But he dismissed it instantly. In his own singleness of heart he could not believe such duplicity possible. Still, it was not without anxiety that he waited to hear what would be said next.

"Well," said Mr. Mudge, slowly, "I don't know but he is a little PEAKED. He's been sick lately, and that's took off his flesh."

"Was he your son?" asked John, in a sympathizing tone; "you must feel quite troubled about him."

He looked askance at Mr. Mudge, enjoying that gentleman's growing irritation.

"My son? No. Where——"

"Nephews perhaps?" suggested the imperturbable John, leisurely continuing the manufacture of a whistle.

"No, I tell you, nothing of the kind. But I can't sit waiting here."

"Oh, I hope you'll excuse me," said John, apologetically. "I hope you won't stop on my account. I didn't know you were in a hurry."

"Well, you know it now," said Mr. Mudge, crossly. "When and where did you see the boy you have described? I am in pursuit of him."

"Has he run away?" inquired John in assumed surprise.

"Are you going to answer my question or not?" demanded Mr. Mudge, angrily.

"Oh, I beg your pardon. I shouldn't have asked so many questions, only I thought he was a nice-looking boy, and I felt interested in him."

"He's a young scamp," said Mr. Mudge, impetuously, "and it's my belief that you're another. Now answer my question. When and where did you see this boy?"

This time Mr. Mudge's menacing look warned John that he had gone far enough. Accordingly he answered promptly, "He passed by our farm this morning."

"How far back is that?"

"About three miles."

"Did he stop there?"

"Yes, he stopped a while to rest."

"Have you seen him since?"

"Yes, I saw him about half a mile back."

"On this road?"

"Yes, but he turned up the road that branches off there."

"Just what I wanted to find out," said Mr. Mudge, in a tone of satisfaction, "I'm sure to catch him."

So saying, he turned about and put his horse to its utmost speed, determined to make up for lost time. When he was fairly out of sight, Paul came forth from his hiding-place.

"How could you do so!" he asked in a reproachful tone.

"Could I do what?" asked John, turning a laughing face towards Paul. "Didn't I tell old Mudge the exact truth? You know you did turn up that road. To be sure you didn't go two rods before turning back. But he didn't stop to ask about that.

If he hadn't been in such a hurry, perhaps I should have told him. Success to him!"

"You can't think how I trembled when you described me so particularly."

"You didn't think I would betray you?" said John, quickly.

"No, but I was afraid you would venture too far, and get us both into trouble."

"Trust me for that, Paul; I've got my eyes wide open, and ain't easily caught. But wasn't it fun to see old Mudge fuming while I kept him waiting. What would he have said if he had known the bird was so near at hand? He looked foolish enough when I asked him if you were his son."

John sat down and gave vent to his pent-up laughter which he had felt obliged to restrain in the presence of Mr. Mudge. He laughed so heartily that Paul, notwithstanding his recent fright and anxiety, could not resist the infection. Together they laughed, till the very air seemed vocal with merriment.

John was the first to recover his gravity.

"I am sorry, Paul," he said, "but I must bid you good-by. They will miss me from the house. I am glad I have got acquainted with you, and I hope I shall see you again some time before very long. Good-by, Paul."

"Good-by, John."

The two boys shook hands and parted. One went in one direction, the other in the opposite. Each looked back repeatedly till the other was out of sight. Then came over Paul once more a feeling of sadness and desolation, which the high spirits of his companion had for the time kept off. Occasionally he cast a glance backwards, to make sure that Mr. Mudge was not following him. But Paul had no cause to fear on that score. The object of his dread was already some miles distant in a different direction.

For an hour longer, Paul trudged on. He met few persons, the road not being very much frequented. He was now at least twelve miles from his starting-place, and began to feel very sensibly the effects of heat and fatigue combined. He threw himself down upon the grass under the overhanging branches of an apple- tree to rest. After his long walk repose seemed delicious, and with a feeling of exquisite enjoyment he stretched himself out at full length upon the soft turf, and closed his eyes.

Insensibly he fell asleep. How long he slept he could not tell. He was finally roused from his slumber by something cold touching his cheek. Starting up he rubbed his eyes in bewilderment, and gradually became aware that this something was the nose of a Newfoundland dog, whose keen scent had enabled him to discover the whereabouts of the small stock of provisions with which Paul had been supplied by his late companion. Fortunately he awoke in time to save its becoming the prey of its canine visitor.

"I reckon you came nigh losing your dinner," fell upon his ears in a rough but hearty tone.

At the same time he heard the noise of wheels, and looking up, beheld a specimen of a class well known throughout New England —a tin pedler. He was seated on a cart liberally stocked with articles of tin ware. From the rear depended two immense bags, one of which served as a receptacle for white rags, the other for bits of calico and whatever else may fall under the designation of "colored." His shop, for such it was, was drawn at a brisk pace by a stout horse, who in this respect presented a contrast to his master, who was long and lank. The pedler himself was a man of perhaps forty, with a face in which shrewdness and good humor seemed alike indicated. Take him for all in all, you might travel some distance without falling in with a more complete specimen of the Yankee.

"So you came nigh losing your dinner," he repeated, in a pleasant tone.

"Yes," said Paul, "I got tired and fell asleep, and I don't know when I should have waked up but for your dog."

"Yes, Boney's got a keen scent for provisions," laughed the pedler. "He's a little graspin', like his namesake. You see his real name is Bonaparte; we only call him Boney, for short."

Meanwhile he had stopped his horse. He was about to start afresh, when a thought struck him.

"Maybe you're goin' my way," said he, turning to Paul; "if you are, you're welcome to a ride."

Paul was very glad to accept the invitation. He clambered into the cart, and took a seat behind the pedler, while Boney, who took his recent disappointment very good-naturedly, jogged on contentedly behind.

"How far are you goin'?" asked Paul's new acquaintance, as he whipped up his horse.

Paul felt a little embarrassed. If he had been acquainted with the names of any of the villages on the route he might easily have answered. As it was, only one name occurred to him.

"I think," said he, with some hesitation, "that I shall go to New York."

"New York!" repeated the pedler, with a whistle expressive of his astonishment.

"Well, you've a journey before you. Got any relations there?"

"No."

"No uncles, aunts, cousins, nor nothing?"

Paul shook his head.

"Then what makes you go? Haven't run away from your father and mother, hey?" asked the pedler, with a knowing look.

"I have no father nor mother," said Paul, sadly enough.

"Well, you had somebody to take care of you, I calculate. Where did you live?"

"If I tell you, you won't carry me back?" said Paul, anxiously.

"Not a bit of it. I've got too much business on hand for that."

Relieved by this assurance, Paul told his story, encouraged thereto by frequent questions from his companion, who seemed to take a lively interest in the adventures of his young companion.

"That's a capital trick you played on old Mudge," he said with a hearty laugh which almost made the tins rattle. "I don't blame you a bit for running away. I've got a story to tell you about Mrs. Mudge. She's a regular skinflint."

XI.

WAYSIDE GOSSIP.

This was the pedler's promised story about Mrs. Mudge.

"The last time I was round that way, I stopped, thinking maybe they might have some rags to dispose of for tin-ware. The old lady seemed glad to see me, and pretty soon she brought down a lot of white rags. I thought they seemed quite heavy for their bulk,— howsomever, I wasn't looking for any tricks, and I let it go. By-and-by, when I happened to be ransacking one of the bags, I came across half a dozen pounds or more of old iron tied up in a white cloth. That let the cat out of the bag. I knew why they were so heavy, then, I reckon I shan't call on Mrs. Mudge next time I go by."

"So you've run off," he continued, after a pause, "I like your spunk,—just what I should have done myself. But tell me how you managed to get off without the old chap's finding it out."

Paul related such of his adventures as he had not before told, his companion listening with marked approval.

"I wish I'd been there," he said. "I'd have given fifty cents, right out, to see how old Mudge looked, I calc'late he's pretty well tired with his wild-goose chase by this time."

It was now twelve o'clock, and both the travelers began to feel the pangs of hunger.

"It's about time to bait, I calc'late," remarked the pedler.

The unsophisticated reader is informed that the word "bait," in New England phraseology, is applied to taking lunch or dining.

At this point a green lane opened out of the public road, skirted on either side by a row of trees. Carpeted with green, it made a very pleasant dining-room. A red-and-white heifer browsing at a little distance looked up from her meal and surveyed the intruders with mild attention, but apparently satisfied that they contemplated no invasion of her rights, resumed her agreeable employment. Over an irregular stone wall our travelers looked into a thrifty apple-orchard laden with fruit. They halted beneath a spreading chestnut-tree which towered above its neighbors, and offered them a grateful shelter from the noonday sun.

From the box underneath the seat, the pedler took out a loaf of bread, a slice of butter, and a tin pail full of doughnuts. Paul, on his side, brought out his bread and gingerbread.

"I most generally carry round my own provisions," remarked the pedler, between two mouthfuls. "It's a good deal cheaper and more convenient, too. Help yourself to the doughnuts. I always calc'late to have some with me. I'd give more for 'em any day than for rich cake that ain't fit for anybody. My mother used to beat everybody in the neighborhood on making doughnuts. She made 'em so good that we never knew when to stop eating. You wouldn't hardly believe it, but, when I was a little shaver, I remember eating twenty- three doughnuts at one time. Pretty nigh killed me."

"I should think it might," said Paul, laughing.

"Mother got so scared that she vowed she wouldn't fry another for three months, but I guess she kinder lost the run of the almanac, for in less than a week she turned out about a bushel more."

All this time the pedler was engaged in practically refuting the saying, that a man cannot do two things at once. With a little assistance from Paul, the stock of doughnuts on which he had been lavishing encomiums, diminished rapidly. It was evident that his attachment to this homely article of diet was quite as strong as ever.

"Don't be afraid of them," said he, seeing that Paul desisted from his efforts, "I've got plenty more in the box."

Paul signified that his appetite was already appeased.

"Then we might as well be jogging on. Hey, Goliah," said he, addressing the horse, who with an air of great content, had been browsing while his master was engaged in a similar manner. "Queer name for a horse, isn't it? I wanted something out of the common way, so I asked mother for a name, and she gave me that. She's great on scripture names, mother is. She gave one to every one of her children. It didn't make much difference to her what they were as long as they were in the Bible. I believe she used to open the Bible at random, and take the first name she happened to come across. There are eight of us, and nary a decent name in the lot. My oldest brother's name is Abimelech. Then there's Pharaoh, and Ishmael, and Jonadab, for the boys, and Leah and Naomi, for the girls; but my name beats all. You couldn't guess it?"

Paul shook his head.

"I don't believe you could," said the pedler, shaking his head in comic indignation. "It's Jehoshaphat. Ain't that a respectable name for the son of Christian parents?"

Paul laughed.

"It wouldn't be so bad," continued the pedler, "if my other name was longer; but Jehoshaphat seems rather a long handle to put before Stubbs. I can't say I feel particularly proud of the name, though for use it'll do as well as any other. At any rate, it ain't quite so bad as the name mother pitched on for my youngest sister, who was lucky enough to die before she needed a name."

"What was it?" inquired Paul, really curious to know what name could be considered less desirable than Jehoshaphat.

"It was Jezebel," responded the pedler.

"Everybody told mother 'twould never do; but she was kind of superstitious about it, because that was the first name she came to in the Bible, and so she thought it was the Lord's will that that name should be given to the child."

As Mr. Stubbs finished his disquisition upon names, there came in sight a small house, dark and discolored with age and neglect. He pointed this out to Paul with his whip-handle.

"That," said he, "is where old Keziah Onthank lives. Ever heard of him?"

Paul had not.

"He's the oldest man in these parts," pursued his loquacious companion. "There's some folks that seem a dyin' all the time, and for all that manage to outlive half the young folks in the neighborhood. Old Keziah Onthank is a complete case in p'int. As long ago as when I was cutting my teeth he was so old that nobody know'd how old he was. He was so bowed over that he couldn't see himself in the looking-glass unless you put it on the floor, and I guess even then what he saw wouldn't pay him for his trouble. He was always ailin' some way or other. Now it was rheumatism, now the palsy, and then again the asthma. He had THAT awful.

"He lived in the same tumble-down old shanty we have just passed,—so poor that nobody'd take the gift of it. People said that he'd orter go to the poorhouse, so that when he was sick—which was pretty much all the time —he'd have some-body to take care of him. But he'd got kinder attached to the old place, seein' he was born there, and never lived anywhere else, and go he wouldn't.

"Everybody expected he was near his end, and nobody'd have been surprised to hear of his death at any minute. But it's strange how some folks are determined to live on, as I said before. So Keziah, though he looked so old when I was a boy that it didn't seem as if he could look any older, kept on livin,' and livin', and arter I got married to Betsy Sprague, he was livin' still.

"One day, I remember I was passin' by the old man's shanty, when I heard a dread-ful groanin', and thinks I to myself, 'I shouldn't wonder if the old man was on his last legs.' So in I bolted. There he was, to be sure, a lyin', on the bed, all curled up into a heap, breathin' dreadful hard, and lookin' as white and pale as any ghost. I didn't know exactly what to do, so I went and got some water, but he motioned it away, and wouldn't drink it, but kept on groanin'.

"'He mustn't be left here to die without any assistance,' thinks I, so I ran off as fast I could to find the doctor.

"I found him eatin' dinner——

"Come quick," says I, "to old Keziah Onthank's. He's dyin', as sure as my name is Jehoshaphat."

"Well," said the doctor, "die or no die, I can't come till I've eaten my dinner."

"But he's dyin', doctor."

"Oh, nonsense. Talk of old Keziah Onthank's dyin'. He'll live longer than I shall."

"I recollect I thought the doctor very unfeelin' to talk so of a fellow creetur, just stepping into eternity, as a body may say. However, it's no use drivin' a horse that's made up his mind he won't go, so although I did think the doctor dreadful deliberate about eatin' his dinner (he always would take half an hour for it), I didn't dare to say a word for fear he wouldn't come at all. You see the doctor was dreadful independent, and was bent on havin' his own way, pretty much, though for that matter I think it's the case with most folks. However, to come back to my story, I didn't feel particularly comfortable while I was waitin' his motions.

"After a long while the doctor got ready. I was in such a hurry that I actilly pulled him along, he walked so slow; but he only laughed, and I couldn't help thinkin' that doctorin' had a hardinin' effect on the heart. I was determined if ever I fell sick I wouldn't send for him.

"At last we got there. I went in all of a tremble, and crept to the bed, thinkin' I should see his dead body. But he wasn't there at all. I felt a little bothered you'd better believe."

"Well," said the doctor, turning to me with a smile, "what do you think now?"

"I don't know what to think," said I.

"Then I'll help you," said he.

"So sayin', he took me to the winder, and what do you think I see? As sure as I'm alive, there was the old man in the back yard, a squattin' down and pickin' up chips."

"And is he still living?"

"Yes, or he was when I come along last. The doctor's been dead these ten years. He told me old Keziah would outlive him, but I didn't believe him. I shouldn't be surprised if he lived forever."

Paul listened with amused interest to this and other stories with which his companion beguiled the way. They served to divert his mind from the realities of his condition, and the uncertainty which hung over his worldly prospects.

XII.

ON THE BRINK OF DISCOVERY.

"If you're in no great hurry to go to New York," said the pedler, "I should like to have you stay with me for a day or two. I live about twenty-five miles from here, straight ahead, so it will be on your way. I always manage to get home by Saturday night if it is any way possible. It doesn't seem comfortable to be away Sunday. As to-day is Friday, I shall get there to-morrow. So you can lie over a day and rest yourself."

Paul felt grateful for this unexpected invitation. It lifted quite a load from his mind, since, as the day declined, certain anxious thoughts as to where he should find shelter, had obtruded themselves. Even now, the same trouble would be experienced on Monday night, but it is the characteristic of youth to pay little regard to anticipated difficulties as long as the present is provided for.

It must not be supposed that the pedler neglected his business on account of his companion. On the road he had been traveling the houses were few and far between. He had, therefore, but few calls to make. Paul remarked, however, that when he did call he seldom failed to sell something.

"Yes," said Mr. Stubbs, on being interrogated, "I make it a p'int to sell something, if it's no more than a tin dipper. I find some hard cases sometimes, and some-times I have to give it up altogether. I can't quite come up to a friend of mine, Daniel Watson, who used to be in the same line of business. I never knew him to stop at a place without selling something. He had a good deal of judgment,

Daniel had, and knew just when to use 'soft sodder,' and when not to. On the road that he traveled there lived a widow woman, who had the reputation of being as ugly, cross- grained a critter as ever lived. People used to say that it was enough to turn milk sour for her even to look at it. Well, it so happened that Daniel had never called there. One night he was boasting that he never called at a house without driving a bargain, when one of the company asked him, with a laugh, if he had ever sold the widow anything. "Why, no," said Daniel, "I never called there; but I've no doubt I could."

"What'll you bet of it?"

"I'm not a betting man," said Daniel, "but I feel so sure of it that I don't mind risking five dollars."

"Agreed."

"The next morning Daniel drove leisurely up to the widow's door and knocked. She had a great aversion to pedlers, and declared they were cheats, every one of them. She was busy sweeping when Daniel knocked. She came to the door in a dreadful hurry, hoping it might be an old widower in the neighborhood that she was trying to catch. When she saw how much she was mistaken she looked as black as a thundercloud.

"Want any tin ware to-day, ma'am?" inquired Daniel, noways discomposed.

"No, sir," snapped she.

"Got all kinds,—warranted the best in the market. Couldn't I sell you something?"

"Not a single thing," said she, preparing to shut the door; but Daniel, knowing all would then be lost, stepped in before she could shut it quite to, and began to name over some of the articles he had in his wagon.

"You may talk till doomsday," said the widow, as mad as could be, "and it won't do a particle of good. Now, you've got your answer, and you'd better leave the house before you are driven out."

"Brooms, brushes, lamps——"

"Here the widow, who had been trying to keep in her anger, couldn't hold out any longer. She seized the broom she had been sweeping with, and brought it down with a tremendous whack upon Daniel's back. You can imagine how hard it was, when I tell you that the force of the blow snapped the broom in the middle. You might have thought Daniel would resent it, but he didn't appear to notice it, though it must have hurt him awful. He picked up the pieces, and handing them, with a polite bow, to the widow, said, "Now, ma'am, I'm sure you need a new broom. I've got some capital ones out in the cart."

"The widow seemed kind of overpowered by his coolness. She hardly knew what to say or what to think. However, she had broken her old broom, that was certain, and must have a new one; so when Daniel ran out and brought in a bundle of them, she picked out one and paid for it without saying a word; only, when Daniel asked if he might have the pleasure of calling again, she looked a little queer, and told him that if he considered it a pleasure, she had no objection."

"And did he call again?"

"Yes, whenever he went that way. The widow was always very polite to him after that, and, though she had a mortal dislike to pedlers in general, she was always ready to trade with him. Daniel used to say that he gained his bet and the widow's custom at ONE BLOW."

They were now descending a little hill at the foot of which stood a country tavern. Here Mr. Stubbs declared his intention of spending the night. He drove into the barn, the large door of which stood invitingly open, and unharnessed his horse, taking especial care to rub him down and set before him an ample supply of provender.

"I always take care of Goliah myself," said he. "He's a good friend to me, and it's no more than right that I should take good care of him. Now, we'll go into the house, and see what we can get for supper."

He was surprised to see that Paul hung back, and seemed disinclined to follow.

"What's the matter?" asked Mr. Stubbs, in surprise. "Why don't you come?"

"Because," said Paul, looking embarrassed, "I've got no money."

"Well, I have," said Mr. Stubbs, "and that will answer just as well, so come along, and don't be bashful. I'm about as hungry as a bear, and I guess you are too."

Before many minutes, Paul sat down to a more bountiful repast than he had partaken of for many a day. There were warm biscuits and fresh butter, such as might please the palate of an epicure, while at the other end of the table was a plate of cake, flanked on one side by an apple-pie, on the other by one of pumpkin, with its rich golden hue, such as is to be found in its perfection, only in New England. It will scarcely be doubted that our hungry travellers did full justice to the fare set before them.

When they had finished, they went into the public room, where were engaged some of the village worthies, intent on discussing the news and the political questions of the day. It was a time of considerable political excitement, and this naturally supplied the topic of conversation. In this the pedler joined, for his frequent travel on this route had made him familiarly acquainted with many of those present.

Paul sat in a corner, trying to feel interested in the conversation; but the day had been a long one, and he had undergone an unusual amount of fatigue. Gradually, his drowsiness increased. The many voices fell upon his ears like a lullaby, and in a few minutes he was fast asleep.

Early next morning they were up and on their way. It was the second morning since Paul's departure. Already a sense of freedom gave his spirits unwonted elasticity, and encouraged him to hope for the best. Had his knowledge of the future been greater, his confidence might have been less. But would he have been any happier?

So many miles separated him from his late home, that he supposed himself quite safe from detection. A slight circumstance warned him that he must still be watchful and cautious.

As they were jogging easily along, they heard the noise of wheels at a little distance. Paul looked up. To his great alarms he recognized in the driver of the approaching vehicle, one of the selectmen of Wrenville.

"What's the matter?" asked his companion, noticing his sudden look of apprehension.

Paul quickly communicated the ground of his alarm.

"And you are afraid he will want to carry you back, are you?"

"Yes."

"Not a bit of it. We'll circumvent the old fellow, unless he's sharper than I think he is. You've only got to do as I tell you."

To this Paul quickly agreed.

The selectman was already within a hundred rods. He had not yet apparently noticed the pedler's cart, so that this was in our hero's favor. Mr. Stubbs had already arranged his plan of operations.

"This is what you are to do, Paul," said he, quickly. "Cock your hat on the side of your head, considerably forward, so that he can't see much of your face. Then here's a cigar to stick in your mouth. You can make believe that you are smoking. If you are the sort of boy I reckon you are, he'll never think it's you."

Paul instantly adopted this suggestion.

Slipping his hat to one side in the jaunty manner characteristic of young America, he began to puff very gravely at a cigar the pedler handed him, frequently taking it from his mouth, as he had seen older persons do, to knock away the ashes. Nothwithstanding his alarm, his love of fun made him enjoy this little stratagem, in which he bore his part successfully.

The selectman eyed him intently. Paul began to tremble from fear of discovery, but his apprehensions were speedily dissipated by a remark of the new-comer, "My boy, you are forming a very bad habit."

Paul did not dare to answer lest his voice should betray him. To his relief, the pedler spoke——

"Just what I tell him, sir, but I suppose he thinks he must do as his father does."

By this time the vehicles had passed each other, and the immediate peril was over.

"Now, Paul," said his companion, laughing, "I'll trouble you for that cigar, if you have done with it. The old gentleman's advice was good. If I'd never learned to smoke, I wouldn't begin now."

Our hero was glad to take the cigar from his mouth. The brief time he had held it was sufficient to make him slightly dizzy.

XIII.

PAUL REACHES THE CITY.

Towards evening they drew up before a small house with a neat yard in front.

"I guess we'll get out here," said Mr. Stubbs. "There's a gentleman lives here that I feel pretty well acquainted with. Shouldn't wonder if he'd let us stop over Sunday. Whoa, Goliah, glad to get home, hey?" as the horse pricked up his ears and showed manifest signs of satisfaction.

"Now, youngster, follow me, and I guess I can promise you some supper, if Mrs. Stubbs hasn't forgotten her old tricks."

They passed through the entry into the kitchen, where Mrs. Stubbs was discovered before the fire toasting slices of bread.

"Lor, Jehoshaphat," said she, "I didn't expect you so soon," and she looked inquiringly at his companion.

"A young friend who is going to stay with us till Monday," explained the pedler. "His name is Paul Prescott."

"I'm glad to see you, Paul," said Mrs. Stubbs with a friendly smile. "You must be tired if you've been traveling far. Take a seat. Here's a rocking-chair for you."

This friendly greeting made Paul feel quite at home. Having no children, the pedler and his wife exerted themselves to make the time pass pleasantly to their young acquaintance. Paul could not help contrasting them with Mr. and Mrs. Mudge, not very much to the advantage of the latter. On Sunday he went to church with them, and the peculiar circumstances in which he was placed, made him listen to the sermon with unusual attention. It was an exposition of the text, "My help cometh from the Lord," and Paul could not help feeling that it was particularly applicable to his own case. It encouraged him to hope, that, however uncertain his prospects appeared, God would help him if he put his trust in Him.

On Monday morning Paul resumed his journey, with an ample stock of provisions supplied by Mrs. Stubbs, in the list of which doughnuts occupied a prominent place; this being at the particular suggestion of Mr. Stubbs.

Forty or fifty miles remained to be traversed before his destination would be reached. The road was not a difficult one to find, and he made it out without much questioning. The first night, he sought permission to sleep in a barn.

He met with a decided refusal.

He was about to turn away in disappointment, when he was called back.

"You are a little too fast, youngster. I said I wouldn't let you sleep in my barn, and I won't; but I've got a spare bed in the house, and if you choose you shall occupy it."

Under the guise of roughness, this man had a kind heart. He inquired into the particulars of Paul's story, and at the conclusion terrified him by saying that he had been very foolish and ought to be sent back. Nevertheless, when Paul took leave of him the next morning, he did not go away empty-handed.

"If you must be so foolish as to set up for yourself, take this," said the farmer, placing half a dollar in his hand. "You may reach the city after the banks are closed for the day, you know," he added, jocularly.

But it was in the morning that Paul came in sight of the city. He climbed up into a high tree, which, having the benefit of an elevated situation, afforded him an extensive prospect. Before him lay the great city of which he had so often heard, teeming with life and activity.

Half in eager anticipation, half in awe and wonder at its vastness, our young pilgrim stood upon the threshold of this great Babel.

Everything looked new and strange. It had never entered Paul's mind, that there could be so many houses in the whole State as now rose up before him. He got into Broadway, and walked on and on thinking that the street must end somewhere. But the farther he walked the thicker the houses seemed crowded together. Every few rods, too, he came to a cross street, which seemed quite as densely peopled as the one on which he was walking. One part of the city was the same as another to Paul, since he was equally a stranger to all. He wandered listlessly along, whither fancy led. His mind was constantly excited by the new and strange objects which met him at every step.

As he was looking in at a shop window, a boy of about his own age, stopped and inquired confidentially, "when did you come from the country?"

"This morning," said Paul, wondering how a stranger should know that he was a country boy.

"Could you tell me what is the price of potatoes up your way?" asked the other boy, with perfect gravity.

"I don't know," said Paul, innocently.

"I'm sorry for that," said the other, "as I have got to buy some for my wife and family."

Paul stared in surprise for a moment, and then realizing that he was being made game of, began to grow angry.

"You'd better go home to your wife and family," he said with spirit, "or you may get hurt."

"Bully for you, country!" answered the other with a laugh. "You're not as green as you look."

"Thank you," said Paul, "I wish I could say as much for you."

Tired with walking, Paul at length sat down in a doorway, and watched with interest the hurrying crowds that passed before him. Everybody seemed to be in a hurry, pressing forward as if life and death depended on his haste. There were lawyers with their sharp, keen glances; merchants with calculating faces; speculators pondering on the chances of a rise or fall in stocks; errand boys with bundles under their arms; business men hurrying to the slip to take the boat for Brooklyn or Jersey City,—all seemed intent on business of some kind, even to the ragged newsboys who had just obtained their supply of evening papers, and were now crying them at the top of their voices,—and very discordant ones at that, so Paul thought. Of the hundreds passing and repassing before him, every one had something to do. Every one had a home to go to. Perhaps it was not altogether strange that a feeling of desolation should come over Paul as he recollected that he stood alone, homeless, friendless, and, it might be, shelterless for the coming night.

"Yet," thought he with something of hopefulness, "there must be something for me to do as well as the rest."

Just then a boy some two years older than Paul paced slowly by, and in passing, chanced to fix his eyes upon our hero. He probably saw something in Paul which attracted him, for he stepped up and extending his hand, said, "why, Tom, how came you here?"

"My name isn't Tom," said Paul, feeling a little puzzled by this address.

"Why, so it isn't. But you look just like my friend, Tom Crocker."

To this succeeded a few inquiries, which Paul unsuspiciously answered.

"Do you like oysters?" inquired the new comer, after a while.

"Very much."

"Because I know of a tip top place to get some, just round the corner. Wouldn't you like some?"

Paul thanked his new acquaintance, and said he would.

Without more ado, his companion ushered him into a basement room near by. He led the way into a curtained recess, and both boys took seats one on each side of a small table.

"Just pull the bell, will you, and tell the waiter we'll have two stews."

Paul did so.

"I suppose," continued the other, "the governor wouldn't like it much if he knew where I was."

"The governor!" repeated Paul. "Why, it isn't against the laws, is it?"

"No," laughed the 'other. "I mean my father. How jolly queer you are!" He meant to say green, but had a purpose in not offending Paul.

"Are you the Governor's son?" asked Paul in amazement.

"To be sure," carelessly replied the other.

Paul's wonder had been excited many times in the course of the day, but this was more surprising than anything which had yet befallen him. That he should have the luck to fall in with the son of the Governor, on his first arrival in the city, and that the latter should prove so affable and condescending, was indeed surprising. Paul inwardly determined to mention it in his first letter to Aunt Lucy. He could imagine her astonishment.

While he was busy with these thoughts, his companion had finished his oysters.

"Most through?" he inquired nonchalantly.

"I've got to step out a minute; wait till I come back."

Paul unsuspectingly assented.

He heard his companion say a word to the barkeeper, and then go out.

He waited patiently for fifteen minutes and he did not return; another quarter of an hour, and he was still absent. Thinking he might have been unexpectedly detained, he rose to go, but was called back by the barkeeper.

"Hallo, youngster! are you going off without paying?"

"For what?" inquired Paul, in surprise.

"For the oysters, of course. You don't suppose I give 'em away, do you?"

"I thought," hesitated Paul, "that the one who was with me paid,—the Governor's son," he added, conscious of a certain pride in his intimacy with one so nearly related to the chief magistrate of the Commonwealth.

"The Governor's son," laughed the barkeeper. "Why the Governor lives a hundred miles off and more. That wasn't the Governor's son any more than I am."

"He called his father governor," said Paul, beginning to be afraid that he had made some ridiculous blunder.

"Well, I wouldn't advise you to trust him again, even if he's the President's son. He only got you in here to pay for his oysters. He told me when he went out that you would pay for them."

"And didn't he say he was coming back?" asked Paul, quite dumbfounded.

"He said you hadn't quite finished, but would pay for both when you came out. It's two shillings.

Paul rather ruefully took out the half dollar which constituted his entire stock of money, and tendered it to the barkeeper who returned him the change.

So Paul went out into the streets, with his confidence in human nature somewhat lessened.

Here, then, is our hero with twenty-five cents in his pocket, and his fortune to make.

XIV.

A STRANGE BED-CHAMBER.

Although Paul could not help being vexed at having been so cleverly taken in by his late companion, he felt the better for having eaten the oysters. Carefully depositing his only remaining coin in his pocket, he resumed his wanderings. It is said that a hearty meal is a good promoter of cheerfulness. It was so in Paul's case, and although he had as yet had no idea where he should find shelter for the night he did not allow that consideration to trouble him.

So the day passed, and the evening came on. Paul's appetite returned to him once more. He invested one-half of his money at an old woman's stall for cakes and apples, and then he ate leisurely while leaning against the iron railing which encircles the park.

He began to watch with interest the movements of those about him. Already the lamplighter had started on his accustomed round, and with ladder in hand was making his way from one lamp-post to another. Paul quite marvelled at the celerity with which the lamps were lighted, never before having witnessed the use of gas. He was so much interested in the process that he sauntered along behind the lamplighter for some time. At length his eye fell upon a group common enough in our cities, but new to him.

An Italian, short and dark-featured, with a velvet cap, was grinding out music from a hand-organ, while a woman with a complexion equally dark, and black sorrowful-looking eyes, accompanied her husband on the tambourine. They were playing a lively tune as Paul came up, but quickly glided into "Home, Sweet Home."

Paul listened with pleased, yet sad interest, for him "home" was only a sad remembrance.

He wandered on, pausing now and then to look into one of the brilliantly illuminated shop windows, or catching a glimpse through the open doors of the gay scene within, and as one after another of these lively scenes passed before him, he began to think that all the strange and wonderful things in the world must be collected in these rich stores.

Next, he came to a place of public amusement. Crowds were entering constantly, and Paul, from curiosity, entered too. He passed on to a little wicket, when a man stopped him.

"Where's your ticket?" he asked.

"I haven't got any," said Paul.

"Then what business have you here?" said the man, roughly.

"Isn't this a meeting-house?" asked Paul.

This remark seemed to amuse two boys who were standing by. Looking up with some indignation, Paul recognized in one of them the boy who had cheated him out of the oysters.

'Look here," said Paul, "what made you go off and leave me to pay for the oysters this morning?"

"Which of us do you mean?" inquired the "governor's son," carelessly.

"I mean you."

"Really, I don't understand your meaning. Perhaps you mistake me for somebody else."

"What?" said Paul, in great astonishment. "Don't you remember me, and how you told me you were the Governor's son?"

Both boys laughed.

"You must be mistaken. I haven't the honor of being related to the distinguished gentleman you name."

The speaker made a mocking bow to Paul.

"I know that," said Paul, with spirit, "but you said you were, for all that."

"It must have been some other good-looking boy, that you are mistaking me for. What are you going to do about it? I hope, by the way, that the oysters agreed with you."

"Yes, they did," said Paul, "for I came honestly by them."

"He's got you there, Gerald," said the other boy.

Paul made his way out of the theater. As his funds were reduced to twelve cents, he could not have purchased a ticket if he had desired it.

Still he moved on.

Soon he came to another building, which was in like manner lighted up, but not so brilliantly as the theater. This time, from the appearance of the building, and from the tall steeple,—so tall that his eye could scarcely reach the tapering spire,—he knew that it must be a church. There was not such a crowd gathered about the door as at the place he had just left, but he saw a few persons entering, and he joined them. The interior of the church was far more gorgeous than the plain village meeting-house which he had been accustomed to attend with his mother. He gazed about him with a feeling of awe, and sank quietly into a back pew. As it was a week-day evening, and nothing of unusual interest was anticipated, there were but few present, here and there one, scattered through the capacious edifice.

By-and-by the organist commenced playing, and a flood of music, grander and more solemn than he had ever heard, filled the whole edifice. He listened with rapt attention and suspended breath till the last note died away, and then sank back upon the richly cushioned seat with a feeling of enjoyment.

In the services which followed he was not so much interested. The officiating clergyman delivered a long homily in a dull unimpassioned manner, which failed to awaken his interest. Already disposed to be drowsy, it acted upon him like a gentle soporific. He tried to pay attention as he had always been used to do, but owing to his occupying a back seat, and the low voice of the preacher, but few words reached him, and those for the most part were above his comprehension.

Gradually the feeling of fatigue—for he had been walking the streets all day— became so powerful that his struggles to keep awake became harder and harder. In vain he sat erect, resolved not to yield. The moment afterwards his head inclined to one side; the lights began to swim before his eyes; the voice of the preacher subsided into a low and undistinguishable hum. Paul's head sank upon the cushion, his bundle, which had been his constant companion during the day, fell softly to the floor, and he fell into a deep sleep.

Meanwhile the sermon came to a close, and another hymn was sung, but even the music was insufficient to wake our hero now. So the benediction was pronounced, and the people opened the doors of their pews and left the church.

Last of all the sexton walked up and down the aisles, closing such of the pew doors as were open. Then he shut off the gas, and after looking around to see that nothing was forgotten, went out, apparently satisfied, and locked the outer door behind him.

Paul, meanwhile, wholly unconscious of his situation, slept on as tranquilly as if there were nothing unusual in the circumstances in which he was placed. Through the stained windows the softened light fell upon his tranquil countenance, on which a smile played, as if his dreams were pleasant. What would Aunt Lucy have thought if she could have seen her young friend at this moment?

XV.

A TURN OF FORTUNE.

Notwithstanding his singular bedchamber, Paul had a refreshing night's sleep from which he did not awake till the sun had fairly risen, and its rays colored by the medium through which they were reflected, streamed in at the windows and rested in many fantastic lines on the richly carved pulpit and luxurious pews.

Paul sprang to his feet and looked around him in bewilderment.

"Where am I?" he exclaimed in astonishment.

In the momentary confusion of ideas which is apt to follow a sudden awakening, he could not remember where he was, or how he chanced to be there. But in a moment memory came to his aid, and he recalled the events of the preceding day, and saw that he must have been locked up in the church.

"How am I going to get out?" Paul asked himself in dismay.

This was the important question just now. He remembered that the village meeting-house which he had been accustomed to attend was rarely opened except on Sundays. What if this should be the case here? It was Thursday morning, and three days must elapse before his release. This would never do. He must seek some earlier mode of deliverance.

He went first to the windows, but found them so secured that it was impossible for him to get them open. He tried the doors, but found, as he had anticipated, that they were fast. His last resource failing, he was at liberty to follow the dictates of his curiosity.

Finding a small door partly open, he peeped within, and found a flight of steep stairs rising before him. They wound round and round, and seemed almost interminable. At length, after he had become almost weary of ascending, he came to a small window, out of which he looked. At his feet lay the numberless roofs of the city, while not far away his eye rested on thousands of masts. The river sparkled in the sun, and Paul, in spite of his concern, could not help enjoying the scene. The sound of horses and carriages moving along the great thoroughfare below came confusedly to his ears. He leaned forward to look down, but the distance was so much greater than he had thought, that he drew back in alarm.

"What shall I do?" Paul asked himself, rather frightened. "I wonder if I can stand going without food for three days? I suppose nobody would hear me if I should scream as loud as I could."

Paul shouted, but there was so much noise in the streets that nobody probably heard him.

He descended the staircase, and once more found himself in the body of the church. He went up into the pulpit, but there seemed no hope of escape in that direction. There was a door leading out on one side, but this only led to a little room into which the minister retired before service.

It semmed rather odd to Paul to find himself the sole occupant of so large a building. He began to wonder whether it would not have been better for him to stay in the poorhouse, than come to New York to die of starvation.

Just at this moment Paul heard a key rattle in the outer door. Filled with new hope, he ran down the pulpit stairs and out into the porch, just in time to see the entrance of the sexton.

The sexton started in surprise as his eye fell upon Paul standing before him, with his bundle under his arm.

"Where did you come from, and how came you here?" he asked with some suspicion.

"I came in last night, and fell asleep."

"So you passed the night here?"

"Yes, sir."

"What made you come in at all?" inquired the sexton, who knew enough of boys to be curious upon this point.

"I didn't know where else to go," said Paul.

"Where do you live?"

Paul answered with perfect truth, "I don't live anywhere."

"What! Have you no home?" asked the sexton in surprise.

Paul shook his head.

"Where should you have slept if you hadn't come in here?"

"I don't know, I'm sure."

"And I suppose you don't know where you shall sleep to-night?"

Paul signified that he did not.

"I knew there were plenty of such cases," said the sexton, meditatively; "but I never seemed to realize it before."

"How long have you been in New York?" was his next inquiry.

"Not very long," said Paul. "I only got here yesterday."

"Then you don't know anybody in the city?"

"No."

"Why did you come here, then?"

"Because I wanted to go somewhere where I could earn a living, and I thought I might find something to do here."

"But suppose you shouldn't find anything to do?"

"I don't know," said Paul, slowly. "I haven't thought much about that."

"Well, my lad," said the sexton, not unkindly, "I can't say your prospects look very bright. You should have good reasons for entering on such an undertaking. I— I don't think you are a bad boy. You don't look like a bad one," he added, half to himself.

"I hope not, sir," said Paul.

"I hope not, too. I was going to say that I wish I could help you to some kind of work. If you will come home with me, you shall be welcome to a dinner, and perhaps I may be able to think of something for you."

Paul gladly prepared to follow his new acquaintance.

"What is your name?" inquired the sexton.

"Paul Prescott."

"That sounds like a good name. I suppose you haven't got much money?"

"Only twelve cents."

"Bless me! only twelve cents. Poor boy! you are indeed poor."

"But I can work," said Paul, spiritedly. "I ought to be able to earn my living."

"Yes, yes, that's the way to feel. Heaven helps those who help themselves."

When they were fairly out of the church, Paul had an opportunity of observing his companion's external appearance. He was an elderly man, with harsh features, which would have been forbidding, but for a certain air of benevolence which softened their expression.

As Paul walked along, he related, with less of detail, the story which is already known to the reader. The sexton said little except in the way of questions designed to elicit further particulars, till, at the conclusion he said, "Must tell Hester."

At length they came to a small house, in a respectable but not fashionable quarter of the city. One-half of this was occupied by the sexton. He opened the door and led the way into the sitting-room. It was plainly but neatly furnished, the only ornament being one or two engravings cheaply framed and hung over the mantel-piece. They were by no means gems of art, but then, the sexton did not claim to be a connoisseur, and would probably not have understood the meaning of the word.

"Sit here a moment," said the sexton, pointing to a chair, "I'll go and speak to Hester."

Paul whiled away the time in looking at the pictures in a copy of "The Pilgrim's Progress," which lay on the table.

In the next room sat a woman of perhaps fifty engaged in knitting. It was very easy to see that she could never have possessed the perishable gift of beauty. Hers was one of the faces on which nature has written PLAIN, in unmistakable characters. Yet if the outward features had been a reflex of the soul within, few faces would have been more attractive than that of Hester Cameron. At the feet of the sexton's wife, for such she was, reposed a maltese cat, purring softly by way of showing her contentment. Indeed, she had good reason to be satisfied. In default of children, puss had become a privileged pet, being well fed and carefully shielded from all the perils that beset cat-hood.

"Home so soon?" said Hester inquiringly, as her husband opened the door.

"Yes, Hester, and I have brought company with me," said the sexton.

"Company!" repeated his wife. "Who is it?"

"It is a poor boy, who was accidentally locked up in the church last night."

"And he had to stay there all night?"

"Yes; but perhaps it was lucky for him, for he had no other place to sleep, and not money enough to pay for one."

"Poor child!" said Hester, compassionately. "Is it not terrible to think that any human creature should be without the comforts of a home which even our tabby possesses. It ought to make you thankful that you are so well cared for, Tab."

The cat opened her eyes and winked drowsily at her mistress.

"So you brought the poor boy home, Hugh?"

"Yes, Hester,—I thought we ought not to begrudge a meal to one less favored by fortune than ourselves. You know we should consider ourselves the almoners of God's bounties."

"Surely, Hugh."

"I knew you would feel so, Hester. And suppose we have the chicken for dinner that I sent in the morning. I begin to have a famous appetite. I think I should enjoy it."

Hester knew perfectly well that it was for Paul's sake, and not for his own, that her husband spoke. But she so far entered into his feelings, that she determined to expend her utmost skill as cook upon the dinner, that Paul might have at least one good meal.

"Now I will bring the boy in," said he. "I am obliged to go to work, but you will find some way to entertain him, I dare say."

"If you will come out (this he said to Paul), I will introduce you to a new friend."

Paul was kindly welcomed by the sexton's wife, who questioned him in a sympathizing tone about his enforced stay in the church. To all her questions Paul answered in a modest yet manly fashion, so as to produce a decidedly favorable impression upon his entertainer.

Our hero was a handsome boy. Just at present he was somewhat thin, not having entirely recovered from the effects of his sickness and poor fare while a member of Mr. Mudge's family; but he was well made, and bade fair to become a stout boy. His manner was free and unembarrassed, and he carried a letter of recommendation in his face. It must be admitted, however that there were two points in which his appearance might have been improved. Both his hands and face had suffered from the dust of travel. His clothes, too, were full of dust.

A single glance told Hester all this, and she resolved to remedy it.

She quietly got some water and a towel, and requested Paul to pull off his jacket, which she dusted while he was performing his ablutions. Then, with the help of a comb to arrange his disordered hair, he seemed quite like a new boy, and felt quite refreshed by the operation.

"Really, it improves him very much," said Hester to herself.

She couldn't help recalling a boy of her own, —the only child she ever had,—who had been accidentally drowned when about the age of Paul.

"If he had only lived," she thought, "how different might have been our lives."

A thought came into her mind, and she looked earnestly at Paul.

"I—yes I will speak to Hugh about it," she said, speaking aloud, unconsciously.

"Did you speak to me?" asked Paul.

"No,—I was thinking of something."

She observed that Paul was looking rather wistfully at a loaf of bread on the table.

"Don't you feel hungry?" she asked, kindly.

"I dare say you have had no breakfast."

"I have eaten nothing since yesterday afternoon."

"Bless my soul! How hungry you must be!" said the good woman, as she bustled about to get a plate of butter and a knife.

She must have been convinced of it by the rapid manner in which the slices of bread and butter disappeared.

At one o'clock the sexton came home. Dinner was laid, and Paul partook of it with an appetite little affected by his lunch of the morning. As he rose from the table, he took his cap, and saying, "Good-by, I thank you very much for your kindness!" he was about to depart.

"Where are you going?" asked the sexton, in surprise.

"I don't know," answered Paul.

"Stop a minute. Hester, I want to speak to you."

They went into the sitting-room together.

"This boy, Hester," he commenced with hesitation.

"Well, Hugh?"

"He has no home."

"It is a hard lot."

"Do you think we should be the worse off if we offered to share our home with him?"

"It is like your kind heart, Hugh. Let us go and tell him."

"We have been talking of you, Paul," said the sexton. "We have thought, Hester and myself, that as you had no home and we no child, we should all be the gainers by your staying with us. Do you consent?"

"Consent!" echoed Paul in joyful surprise. "How can I ever repay your kindness?"

"If you are the boy we take you for, we shall feel abundantly repaid. Hester, we can give Paul the little bedroom where—where John used to sleep."

His voice faltered a little, for John was the name of his boy, who had been drowned.

XVI.

YOUNG STUPID.

Paul found the sexton's dwelling very different from his last home, if the Poorhouse under the charge of Mr. and Mrs. Mudge deserved such a name. His present home was an humble one, but he was provided with every needful comfort, and the atmosphere of kindness which surrounded him, gave him a feeling of peace and happiness which he had not enjoyed for a long time.

Paul supposed that he would be at once set to work, and even then would have accounted himself fortunate in possessing such a home.

But Mr. Cameron had other views for him.

"Are you fond of studying?" asked the sexton, as they were all three gathered in the little sitting room, an evening or two after Paul first came.

"Very much!" replied our hero.

"And would you like to go to school?"

"What, here in New York?"

"Yes."

"Oh, very much indeed."

"I am glad to hear you say so, my lad. There is nothing like a good education. If I had a son of my own, I would rather leave him that than money, for while the last may be lost, the first never can be. And though you are not my son, Paul, Providence has in a manner conducted you to me, and I feel responsible for your future. So you shall go to school next Monday morning, and I hope you will do yourself much credit there."

"Thank you very much," said Paul. "I feel very grateful, but——"

"You surely are not going to object?" said the sexton.

"No, but——"

"Well, Paul, go on," seeing that the boy hesitated. "Why," said our hero, with a sense of delicacy which did him credit, "If I go to school, I shall not be able to earn my board, and shall be living at your expense, though I have no claim upon you."

"Oh, is that all?" said the sexton cheerfully, "I was afraid that it was something more serious. As to that, I am not rich, and never expect to be. But what little expense you will be will not ruin me. Besides, when you are grown up and doing well, you can repay me, if I ever need it."

"That I will," said Paul.

"Mind, if I ever need it,—not otherwise. There, now, it's a bargain on that condition. You haven't any other objection," seeing that Paul still hesitated.

"No, or at least I should like to ask your advice," said Paul. "Just before my father died, he told me of a debt of five hundred dollars which he had not been able to pay. I saw that it troubled him, and I promised to pay it whenever I was able. I don't know but I ought to go to work so as to keep my promise."

"No," said the sexton after a moment's reflection, "the best course will be to go to school, at present. Knowledge is power, and a good education will help you to make money by and by. I approve your resolution, my lad, and if you keep it resolutely in mind I have no doubt you will accomplish your object. But the quickest road to success is through the schoolroom. At present you are not able to earn much. Two or three years hence will be time enough."

Paul's face brightened as the sexton said this. He instinctively felt that Mr. Cameron was right. He had never forgotten his father's dying injunction, and this was one reason that impelled him to run away from the Almshouse, because he felt that while he remained he never would be in a situation to carry out his father's wishes. Now his duty was reconciled with his pleasure, and he gratefully accepted the sexton's suggestions.

The next Monday morning, in accordance with the arrangement which had just been agreed upon, Paul repaired to school. He was at once placed in a class, and lessons were assigned him.

At first his progress was not rapid. While living in Wrenville he had an opportunity only of attending a country school, kept less than six months in the year, and then not affording advantages to be compared with those of a city school. During his father's sickness, besides, he had been kept from school altogether. Of course all this lost time could not be made up in a moment. Therefore it was that Paul lagged behind his class.

There are generally some in every school, who are disposed to take unfair advantage of their schoolmates, or to ridicule those whom they consider inferior to themselves.

There was one such in Paul's class. His name was George Dawkins.

He was rather a showy boy, and learned easily. He might have stood a class above where he was, if he had not been lazy, and depended too much on his natural talent. As it was, he maintained the foremost rank in his class.

"Better be the first man in a village than the second man in Rome," he used to say; and as his present position not only gave him the pre-eminence which he desired, but cost him very little exertion to maintain, he was quite well satisfied with it.

This boy stood first in his class, while Paul entered at the foot.

He laughed unmercifully at the frequent mistakes of our hero, and jeeringly dubbed him, "Young Stupid."

"Do you know what Dawkins calls you?" asked one of the boys.

"No. What does he call me?" asked Paul, seriously.

"He calls you 'Young Stupid.'"

Paul's face flushed painfully. Ridicule was as painful to him as it is to most boys, and he felt the insult deeply.

"I'd fight him if I were you," was the volunteered advice of his informant.

"No," said Paul. "That wouldn't mend the matter. Besides, I don't know but he has some reason for thinking so."

"Don't call yourself stupid, do you?"

"No, but I am not as far advanced as most boys of my age. That isn't my fault, though. I never had a chance to go to school much. If I had been to school all my life, as Dawkins has, it would be time to find out whether I am stupid or not."

"Then you ain't going to do anything about it?"

"Yes, I am."

"You said you wasn't going to fight him."

"That wouldn't do any good. But I'm going to study up and see if I can't get ahead of him. Don't you think that will be the best way of showing him that he is mistaken?"

"Yes, capital, but——"

"But you think I can't do it, I suppose," said Paul.

"You know he is at the head of the class, and you are at the foot."

"I know that," said Paul, resolutely. "But wait awhile and see."

In some way George Dawkins learned that Paul had expressed the determination to dispute his place. It occasioned him considerable amusement.

"Halloa, Young Stupid," he called out, at recess.

Paul did not answer.

"Why don't you answer when you are spoken to?" he asked angrily.

"When you call me by my right name," said Paul, quietly, "I will answer, and not before."

"You're mighty independent," sneered Dawkins. "I don't know but I may have to teach you manners."

"You had better wait till you are qualified," said Paul, coolly.

Dawkins approached our hero menacingly, but Paul did not look in the least alarmed, and he concluded to attack him with words only.

"I understand you have set yourself up as my rival!" he said, mockingly.

"Not just yet," said Paul, "but in time I expect to be."

"So you expect my place," said Dawkins, glancing about him.

"We'll talk about that three months hence," said Paul.

"Don't hurt yourself studying," sneered Dawkins, scornfully.

To this Paul did not deign a reply, but the same day he rose one in his class. Our hero had a large stock of energy and determination. When he had once set his mind upon a thing, he kept steadily at work till he accomplished it. This is the great secret of success. It sometimes happens that a man who has done nothing will at once accomplish a brilliant success by one spasmodic effort, but such cases are extremely rare.

"Slow and sure wins the race," is an old proverb that has a great deal of truth in it.

Paul worked industriously.

The kind sexton and his wife, who noticed his assiduity, strove to dissuade him from working so steadily.

"You are working too hard, Paul," they said.

"Do I look pale?" asked Paul, pointing with a smile to his red cheeks.

"No, but you will before long."

"When I am, I will study less. But you know, Uncle Hugh," so the sexton instructed him to call him, "I want to make the most of my present advantages. Besides, there's a particular boy who thinks I am stupid. I want to convince him that he is mistaken."

"You are a little ambitious, then, Paul?"

"Yes, but it isn't that alone. I know the value of knowledge, and I want to secure as much as I can."

"That is an excellent motive, Paul."

"Then you won't make me study less?"

"Not unless I see you are getting sick."

Paul took good care of this. He knew how to play as well as to study, and his laugh on the playground was as merry as any. His cheerful, obliging disposition made him a favorite with his companions. Only George Dawkins held out; he had, for some reason, inbibed a dislike for Paul.

Paul's industry was not without effect. He gradually gained position in his class.

"Take care, Dawkins," said one of his companions—the same one who had before spoken to Paul—"Paul Prescott will be disputing your place with you. He has come up seventeen places in a month."

"Much good it'll do him," said Dawkins, contemptuously.

"For all that, you will have to be careful; I can tell you that."

"I'm not in the least afraid. I'm a little too firm in my position to be ousted by Young Stupid."

"Just wait and see."

Dawkins really entertained no apprehension. He had unbounded confidence in himself, and felt a sense of power in the rapidity with which he could master a lesson. He therefore did not study much, and though he could not but see that Paul was rapidly advancing, he rejected with scorn the idea that Young Stupid could displace him.

This, however, was the object at which Paul was aiming. He had not forgotten the nickname which Dawkins had given him, and this was the revenge which he sought,—a strictly honorable one.

At length the day of his triumph came. At the end of the month the master read off the class-list, and, much to his disgust, George Dawkins found himself playing second fiddle to Young Stupid.

XVII.

BEN'S PRACTICAL JOKE.

Mrs. Mudge was in the back room, bending over a tub. It was washing-day, and she was particularly busy. She was a driving, bustling woman, and, whatever might be her faults of temper, she was at least industrious and energetic. Had Mr. Mudge been equally so, they would have been better off in a worldly point of view. But her husband was constitutionally lazy, and was never disposed to do more than was needful.

Mrs. Mudge was in a bad humor that morning. One of the cows had got into the garden through a gap in the fence, and made sad havoc among the cabbages. Now if Mrs. Mudge had a weakness, it was for cabbages. She was excessively fond of them, and had persuaded her husband to set out a large number of plants from which she expected a large crop. They were planted in one corner of the garden, adjoining a piece of land, which, since mowing, had been used for pasturing the cows. There was a weak place in the fence separating the two inclosures, and this Mrs. Mudge had requested her husband to attend to. He readily promised this, and Mrs. Mudge supposed it done, until that same morning, her sharp eyes had detected old Brindle munching the treasured cabbages with a provoking air of enjoyment. The angry lady seized a broom, and repaired quickly to the scene of devastation. Brindle scented the danger from afar, and beat a disorderly retreat, trampling down the cabbages which she had hitherto spared. Leaping over the broken fence, she had just cleared the gap as the broom-handle, missing her, came forcibly down upon the rail, and was snapped in sunder by the blow.

Here was a new vexation. Brindle had not only escaped scot-free, but the broom, a new one, bought only the week before, was broken.

"It's a plaguy shame," said Mrs. Mudge, angrily. "There's my best broom broken; cost forty-two cents only last week."

She turned and contemplated the scene of devastation. This yielded her little consolation.

"At least thirty cabbages destroyed by that scamp of a cow," she exclaimed in a tone bordering on despair. "I wish I'd a hit her. If I'd broken my broom over her back I wouldn't a cared so much. And it's all Mudge's fault. He's the most shiftless man I ever see. I'll give him a dressing down, see if I don't."

Mrs. Mudge's eyes snapped viciously, and she clutched the relics of the broom with a degree of energy which rendered it uncertain what sort of a dressing down she intended for her husband.

Ten minutes after she had re-entered the kitchen, the luckless man made his appearance. He wore his usual look, little dreaming of the storm that awaited him.

"I'm glad you've come," said Mrs. Mudge, grimly.

"What's amiss, now?" inquired Mudge, for he understood her look.

"What's amiss?" blazed Mrs. Mudge. "I'll let you know. Do you see this?"

She seized the broken broom and flourished it in his face.

"Broken your broom, have you? You must have been careless."

"Careless, was I?" demanded Mrs. Mudge, sarcastically. "Yes, of course, it's always I that am in fault."

"You haven't broken it over the back of any of the paupers, have you?" asked her husband, who, knowing his helpmeet's infirmity of temper, thought it possible she might have indulged in such an amusement.

"If I had broken it over anybody's back it would have been yours," said the lady.

"Mine! what have I been doing?"

"It's what you haven't done," said Mrs. Mudge. "You're about the laziest and most shiftless man I ever came across."

"Come, what does all this mean?" demanded Mr. Mudge, who was getting a little angry in his turn.

"I'll let you know. Just look out of that window, will you?"

"Well," said Mr. Mudge, innocently, "I don't see anything in particular."

"You don't!" said Mrs. Mudge with withering sarcasm. "Then you'd better put on your glasses. If you'd been here quarter of an hour ago, you'd have seen Brindle among the cabbages."

"Did she do any harm?" asked Mr. Mudge, hastily.

"There's scarcely a cabbage left," returned Mrs. Mudge, purposely exaggerating the mischief done.

"If you had mended that fence, as I told you to do, time and again, it wouldn't have happened."

"You didn't tell me but once," said Mr. Mudge, trying to get up a feeble defence.

"Once should have been enough, and more than enough. You expect me to slave myself to death in the house, and see to all your work besides. If I'd known what a lazy, shiftless man you were, at the time I married you, I'd have cut off my right hand first."

By this time Mr. Mudge had become angry.

"If you hadn't married me, you'd a died an old maid," he retorted.

This was too much for Mrs. Mudge to bear. She snatched the larger half of the broom, and fetched it down with considerable emphasis upon the back of her liege lord, who, perceiving that her temper was up, retreated hastily from the kitchen; as he got into the yard he descried Brindle, whose appetite had been whetted by her previous raid, re-entering the garden through the gap.

It was an unfortunate attempt on the part of Brindle. Mr. Mudge, angry with his wife, and smarting with the blow from the broomstick, determined to avenge himself upon the original cause of all the trouble. Revenge suggested craft. He seized a hoe, and crept stealthily to the cabbage-plot. Brindle, whose back was turned, did not perceive his approach, until she felt a shower of blows upon her back. Confused at the unexpected attack she darted wildly away, forgetting the gap in the fence, and raced at random over beds of vegetables, uprooting beets, parsnips, and turnips, while Mr. Mudge, mad with rage, followed close in her tracks, hitting her with the hoe whenever he got a chance.

Brindle galloped through the yard, and out at the open gate. Thence she ran up the road at the top of her speed, with Mr. Mudge still pursuing her.

It may be mentioned here that Mr. Mudge was compelled to chase the terrified cow over two miles before he succeeded with the help of a neighbor in capturing her. All this took time. Meanwhile Mrs. Mudge at home was subjected to yet another trial of her temper.

It has already been mentioned that Squire Newcome was Chairman of the Overseers of the Poor. In virtue of his office, he was expected to exercise a general supervision over the Almshouse and its management. It was his custom to call about once a month to look after matters, and ascertain whether any official action or interference was needed.

Ben saw his father take his gold-headed cane from behind the door, and start down the road. He understood his destination, and instantly the plan of a stupendous practical joke dawned upon him.

"It'll be jolly fun," he said to himself, his eyes dancing with fun. "I'll try it, anyway."

He took his way across the fields, so as to reach the Almshouse before his father. He then commenced his plan of operations.

Mrs. Mudge had returned to her tub, and was washing away with bitter energy, thinking over her grievances in the matter of Mr. Mudge, when a knock was heard at the front door.

Taking her hands from the tub, she wiped them on her apron.

"I wish folks wouldn't come on washing day!" she said in a tone of vexation.

She went to the door and opened it.

There was nobody there.

"I thought somebody knocked," thought she, a little mystified. "Perhaps I was mistaken."

She went back to her tub, and had no sooner got her hands in the suds than another knock was heard, this time on the back door.

"I declare!" said she, in increased vexation, "There's another knock. I shan't get through my washing to-day."

Again Mrs. Mudge wiped her hands on her apron, and went to the door.

There was nobody there.

I need hardly say that it was Ben, who had knocked both times, and instantly dodged round the corner of the house.

"It's some plaguy boy," said Mrs. Mudge, her eyes blazing with anger. "Oh, if I could only get hold of him!"

"Don't you wish you could?" chuckled Ben to himself, as he caught a sly glimpse of the indignant woman.

Meanwhile, Squire Newcome had walked along in his usual slow and dignified manner, until he had reached the front door of the Poorhouse, and knocked.

"It's that plaguy boy again," said Mrs. Mudge, furiously. "I won't go this time, but if he knocks again, I'll fix him."

She took a dipper of hot suds from the tub in which she had been washing, and crept carefully into the entry, taking up a station close to the front door.

"I wonder if Mrs. Mudge heard me knock," thought Squire Newcome. "I should think she might. I believe I will knock again."

This time he knocked with his cane.

Rat-tat-tat sounded on the door.

The echo had not died away, when the door was pulled suddenly open, and a dipper full of hot suds was dashed into the face of the astonished Squire, accompanied with, "Take that, you young scamp!"

"Wh—what does all this mean?" gasped Squire Newcome, nearly strangled with the suds, a part of which had found its way into his mouth.

"I beg your pardon, Squire Newcome," said the horrified Mrs. Mudge. "I didn't mean it."

"What did you mean, then?" demanded Squire Newcome, sternly. "I think you addressed me,—ahem!—as a scamp."

"Oh, I didn't mean you," said Mrs. Mudge, almost out of her wits with perplexity.

"Come in, sir, and let me give you a towel. You've no idea how I've been tried this morning."

"I trust," said the Squire, in his stateliest tone, "you will be able to give a satisfactory explanation of this, ahem—extraordinary proceeding."

While Mrs. Mudge was endeavoring to sooth the ruffled dignity of the aggrieved Squire, the "young scamp," who had caused all the mischief, made his escape through the fields.

"Oh, wasn't it bully!" he exclaimed. "I believe I shall die of laughing. I wish Paul had been here to see it. Mrs. Mudge has got herself into a scrape, now, I'm thinking."

Having attained a safe distance from the Poorhouse, Ben doubled himself up and rolled over and over upon the grass, convulsed with laughter.

"I'd give five dollars to see it all over again," he said to himself. "I never had such splendid fun in my life."

Presently the Squire emerged, his tall dicky looking decidedly limp and drooping, his face expressing annoyance and outraged dignity. Mrs. Mudge attended him to the door with an expression of anxious concern.

"I guess I'd better make tracks," said Ben to himself, "it won't do for the old gentleman to see me here, or he may smell a rat."

He accordingly scrambled over a stone wall and lay quietly hidden behind it till he judged it would be safe to make his appearance.

XVIII.

MORE ABOUT BEN.

"Benjamin," said Squire Newcome, two days after the occurrence mentioned in the last chapter, "what made the dog howl so this morning? Was you a doing anything to him?"

"I gave him his breakfast," said Ben, innocently. "Perhaps he was hungry, and howling for that."

"I do not refer to that," said the Squire. "He howled as if in pain or terror. I repeat; was you a doing anything to him?"

Ben shifted from one foot to the other, and looked out of the window.

"I desire a categorical answer," said Squire Newcome.

"Don't know what categorical means," said Ben, assuming a perplexed look.

"I desire you to answer me IMMEGIATELY," explained the Squire. "What was you a doing to Watch?"

"I was tying a tin-kettle to his tail," said Ben, a little reluctantly.

"And what was you a doing that for?" pursued the Squire.

"I wanted to see how he would look," said Ben, glancing demurely at his father, out of the corner of his eye.

"Did it ever occur to you that it must be disagreeable to Watch to have such an appendage to his tail?" queried the Squire.

"I don't know," said Ben.

"How should you like to have a tin pail suspended to your—ahem! your coat tail?"

"I haven't got any coat tail," said Ben, "I wear jackets. But I think I am old enough to wear coats. Can't I have one made, father?"

"Ahem!" said the Squire, blowing his nose, "we will speak of that at some future period."

"Fred Newell wears a coat, and he isn't any older than I am," persisted Ben, who was desirous of interrupting his father's inquiries.

"I apprehend that we are wandering from the question," said the Squire. "Would you like to be treated as you treated Watch?"

"No," said Ben, slowly, "I don't know as I should."

"Then take care not to repeat your conduct of this morning," said his father. "Stay a moment," as Ben was about to leave the room hastily. "I desire that you should go to the post-office and inquire for letters."

"Yes, sir."

Ben left the room and sauntered out in the direction of the post-office.

A chaise, driven by a stranger, stopped as it came up with him.

The driver looked towards Ben, and inquired, "Boy, is this the way to Sparta?"

Ben, who was walking leisurely along the path, whistling as he went, never turned his head.

"Are you deaf, boy?" said the driver, impatiently. "I want to know if this is the road to Sparta?"

Ben turned round.

"Fine morning, sir," he said politely.

"I know that well enough without your telling me. Will you tell me whether this is the road to Sparta?"

Ben put his hand to his ear, and seemed to listen attentively. Then he slowly shook his head, and said, "Would you be kind enough to speak a little louder, sir?"

"The boy is deaf, after all," said the driver to himself. "IS THIS THE ROAD TO SPARTA?"

"Yes, sir, this is Wrenville," said Ben, politely.

"Plague take it! he don't hear me yet. IS THIS THE ROAD TO SPARTA?"

"Just a little louder, if you please," said Ben, keeping his hand to his ear, and appearing anxious to hear.

"Deaf as a post!" muttered the driver. "I couldn't scream any louder, if I should try. Go along."

"Poor man! I hope he hasn't injured his voice," thought Ben, his eyes dancing with fun. "By gracious!" he continued a moment later, bursting into a laugh, "if he isn't going to ask the way of old Tom Haven. He's as deaf as I pretended to be."

The driver had reined up again, and inquired the way to Sparta.

"What did you say?" said the old man, putting his hand to his ear. "I'm rather hard of hearing."

The traveller repeated his question in a louder voice.

The old man shook his head.

"I guess you'd better ask that boy," he said, pointing to Ben, who by this time had nearly come up with the chaise.

"I have had enough of him," said the traveller, disgusted. "I believe you're all deaf in this town. I'll get out of it as soon as possible."

He whipped up his horse, somewhat to the old man's surprise, and drove rapidly away.

I desire my young readers to understand that I am describing Ben as he was, and not as he ought to be. There is no doubt that he carried his love of fun too far. We will hope that as he grows older, he will grow wiser.

Ben pursued the remainder of his way to the Post-office without any further adventure.

Entering a small building appropriated to this purpose, he inquired for letters.

"There's nothing for your father to-day," said the post-master.

"Perhaps there's something for me,— Benjamin Newcome, Esq.," said Ben.

"Let me see," said the post-master, putting on his spectacles; "yes, I believe there is. Post-marked at New York, too. I didn't know you had any correspondents there."

"It's probably from the Mayor of New York," said Ben, in a tone of comical importance, "asking my advice about laying out Central Park."

"Probably it is," said the postmaster. "It's a pretty thick letter,—looks like an official document."

By this time, Ben, who was really surprised by the reception of the letter, had opened it. It proved to be from our hero, Paul Prescott, and inclosed one for Aunt Lucy.

"Mr. Crosby," said Ben, suddenly, addressing the postmaster, "you remember about Paul Prescott's running away from the Poorhouse?"

"Yes, I didn't blame the poor boy a bit. I never liked Mudge, and they say his wife is worse than he."

"Well, suppose the town should find out where he is, could they get him back again?"

"Bless you! no. They ain't so fond of supporting paupers. If he's able to earn his own living, they won't want to interfere with him."

"Well, this letter is from him," said Ben. "He's found a pleasant family in New York, who have adopted him."

"I'm glad of it," said Mr. Crosby, heartily. "I always liked him. He was a fine fellow."

"That's just what I think. I'll read his letter to you, if you would like to hear it."

"I should, very much. Come in behind here, and sit down."

Ben went inside the office, and sitting down on a stool, read Paul's letter. As our reader may be interested in the contents, we will take the liberty of looking over Ben's shoulder while he reads.

New York, Oct. 10, 18—.
DEAR BEN:—

I have been intending to write to you before, knowing the kind interest which you take in me. I got safely to New York a few days after I left Wrenville. I didn't have so hard a time as I expected, having fallen in with a pedler, who was very kind to me, with whom I rode thirty or forty miles. I wish I had time to tell all the adventures I met with on the way, but I must wait till I see you.

When I got to the city, I was astonished to find how large it was. The first day I got pretty tired wandering about, and strayed into a church in the evening, not knowing where else to go. I was so tired I fell asleep there, and didn't wake up till morning. When I found myself locked up in a great church, I was frightened, I can tell you. It was only Thursday morning, and I was afraid I should have to stay there till Sunday. If I had, I am afraid I should have starved to death. But, fortunately for me, the sexton came in the morning, and let me out. That wasn't all. He very kindly took me home with him, and then told me I might live with him and go to school. I like him very much, and his wife too. I call them Uncle Hugh and Aunt Hester. When you write to me, you must direct to the care of Mr. Hugh Cameron, 10 R—— Street. Then it will be sure to reach me.

I am going to one of the city schools. At first, I was a good deal troubled because I was so far behind boys of my age. You know I hadn't been to school for a long time before I left Wrenville, on account of father's sickness. But I studied pretty hard, and now I stand very well. I sometimes think, Ben, that you don't care quite so much about study as you ought to. I wish you would come to feel the importance of it. You must excuse me saying this, as we have always been such good friends.

I sometimes think of Mr. and Mrs. Mudge, and wonder whether they miss me much. I am sure Mr. Mudge misses me, for now he is obliged to get up early and milk, unless he has found another boy to do it. If he has, I pity the boy. Write me what they said about my going away.

I inclose a letter for Aunt Lucy Lee, which I should like to have you give her with your own hands. Don't trust it to Mrs. Mudge, for she doesn't like Aunt Lucy, and I don't think she would give it to her.

Write soon, Ben, and I will answer without delay,
Your affectionate friend,
PAUL PRESCOTT.

"That's a very good letter," said Mr. Crosby; "I am glad Paul is doing so well. I should like to see him."

"So should I," said Ben; "he was a prime fellow,—twice as good as I am. That's true, what he said about my not liking study. I guess I'll try to do better."

"You'll make a smart boy if you only try," said the postmaster, with whom Ben was rather a favorite, in spite of his mischievous propensities.

"Thank you," said Ben, laughing, "that's what my friend, the mayor of New York, often writes me. But honestly, I know I can do a good deal better than I am doing now. I don't know but I shall turn over a new leaf. I suppose I like fun a little too well. Such jolly sport as I had coming to the office this morning."

Ben related the story of the traveller who inquired the way to Sparta, much to the amusement of the postmaster, who, in his enjoyment of the joke, forgot to tell Ben that his conduct was hardly justifiable.

"Now," said Ben, "as soon as I have been home, I must go and see my particular friend, Mrs. Mudge. I'm a great favorite of hers," he added, with a sly wink.

XIX.

MRS. MUDGE'S DISCOMFITURE.

Ben knocked at the door of the Poorhouse. In due time Mrs. Mudge appeared. She was a little alarmed on seeing Ben, not knowing how Squire Newcome might be affected by the reception she had given him on his last visit. Accordingly she received him with unusual politeness.

"How do you do, Master Newcome?" she inquired.

"As well as could be expected," said Ben, hesitatingly.

"Why, is there anything the matter with you?" inquired Mrs. Mudge, her curiosity excited by his manner of speaking.

"No one can tell what I suffer from rheumatism," said Ben, sadly.

This was very true, since not even Ben himself could have told.

"You are very young to be troubled in that way," said Mrs. Mudge, "and how is your respected father, to-day?" she inquired, with some anxiety.

"I was just going to ask you, Mrs. Mudge," said Ben, "whether anything happened to disturb him when he called here day before yesterday?"

"Why," said Mrs. Mudge, turning a little pale, "Nothing of any consequence,— that is, not much. What makes you ask?"

"I thought it might be so from his manner," said Ben, enjoying Mrs. Mudge's evident alarm.

"There was a little accident," said Mrs. Mudge, reluctantly. "Some mischievous boy had been knocking and running away; so, when your father knocked, I thought it might be he, and—and I believe I threw some water on him. But I hope he has forgiven it, as it wasn't intentional. I should like to get hold of that boy," said Mrs. Mudge, wrathfully, "I should like to shake him up."

"Have you any idea who it was?" asked Ben, gravely.

"No," said Mrs. Mudge, "I haven't, but I shall try to find out. Whoever it is, he's a scamp."

"Very complimentary old lady," thought Ben. He said in a sober tone, which would have imposed upon any one, "There are a good many mischievous boys around here."

Mrs. Mudge grimly assented.

"Oh, by the way, Mrs. Mudge," asked Ben, suddenly, "have you ever heard anything of Paul Prescott since he left you?"

"No," snapped Mrs. Mudge, her countenance growing dark, "I haven't. But I can tell pretty well where he is."

"Where?"

"In the penitentiary. At any rate, if he isn't, he ought to be. But what was you wanting?"

"I want to see Mrs. Lee."

"Aunt Lucy Lee?"

"Yes. I've got a letter for her."

"If you'll give me the letter I'll carry it to her."

"Thank you," said Ben, "but I would like to see her."

"Never mind," thought Mrs. Mudge, "I'll get hold of it yet. I shouldn't wonder at all if it was from that rascal, Paul."

Poor Paul! It was fortunate that he had some better friends than Mr. and Mrs. Mudge, otherwise he would have been pretty poorly off.

Aunt Lucy came to the door. Ben placed the letter in her hands.

"Is it from Paul?" she asked, hopefully.

"Yes," said Ben.

She opened it eagerly. "Is he well?" she asked.

"Yes, well and happy," said Ben, who treated the old lady, for whom he had much respect, very differently from Mrs. Mudge.

"I'm truly thankful for that," said Aunt Lucy; "I've laid awake more than one night thinking of him."

"So has Mrs. Mudge, I'm thinking," said Ben, slyly.

Aunt Lucy laughed.

"There isn't much love lost between them," said Aunt Lucy, smiling. "He was very badly treated here, poor boy."

"Was he, though?" repeated Mrs. Mudge? who had been listening at the keyhole, but not in an audible voice. "Perhaps he will be again, if I get him back. I thought that letter was from Paul. I must get hold of it some time to-day."

"I believe I must go," said Ben. "If you answer the letter, I will put it into the office for you. I shall be passing here to-morrow."

"You are very kind," said Aunt Lucy. "I am very much obliged to you for bringing me this letter to-day. You can't tell how happy it makes me. I have been so afraid the dear boy might be suffering."

"It's no trouble at all," said Ben.

"She's a pretty good woman," thought he, as he left the house. "I wouldn't play a trick on her for a good deal. But that Mrs. Mudge is a hard case. I wonder what she would have said if she had known that I was the "scamp" that troubled her so much Monday. If I had such a mother as that, by jingo, I'd run away to sea."

Mrs. Mudge was bent upon reading Aunt Lucy's letter. Knowing it to be from Paul, she had a strong curiosity to know what had become of him. If she could only get him back! Her heart bounded with delight as she thought of the annoyances to which, in that case, she could subject him. It would be a double triumph over him and Aunt Lucy, against whom she felt that mean spite with which a superior nature is often regarded by one of a lower order.

After some reflection, Mrs. Mudge concluded that Aunt Lucy would probably leave the letter in the little chest which was appropriated to her use, and which was kept in the room where she slept. The key of this chest had been lost, and although Aunt Lucy had repeatedly requested that a new one should be obtained, Mrs. Mudge had seen fit to pay no attention to her request, as it would interfere with purposes of her own, the character of which may easily be guessed.

As she suspected, Paul's letter had been deposited in this chest.

Accordingly, the same afternoon, she left her work in the kitchen in order to institute a search for it. As a prudent precaution, however, she just opened the door of the common room, to make sure that Aunt Lucy was at work therein.

She made her way upstairs, and entering the room in which the old lady lodged, together with two others, she at once went to the chest and opened it.

She began to rummage round among the old lady's scanty treasures, and at length, much to her joy, happened upon the letter, laid carefully away in one corner of the chest. She knew it was the one she sought, from the recent postmark, and the address, which was in the unformed handwriting of a boy. To make absolutely certain, she drew the letter from the envelope and looked at the signature.

She was right, as she saw at a glance. It was from Paul.

"Now I'll see what the little rascal has to say for himself," she muttered, "I hope he's in distress; oh, how I'd like to get hold of him."

Mrs. Mudge began eagerly to read the letter, not dreaming of interruption. But she was destined to be disappointed. To account for this we must explain that, shortly after Mrs. Mudge looked into the common room, Aunt Lucy was reminded of something essential, which she had left upstairs. She accordingly laid down her work upon the chair in which she had been sitting, and went up to her chamber.

Mrs. Mudge was too much preoccupied to hear the advancing steps.

As the old lady entered the chamber, what was her mingled indignation and dismay at seeing Mrs. Mudge on her knees before _*her_ chest, with the precious letter, whose arrival had gladdened her so much, in her hands.

"What are you doing there, Mrs. Mudge?" she said, sternly.

Mrs. Mudge rose from her knees in confusion. Even she had the grace to be ashamed of her conduct.

"Put down that letter," said the old lady in an authoritative voice quite new to her.

Mrs. Mudge, who had not yet collected her scattered senses, did as she was requested.

Aunt Lucy walked hastily to the chest, and closed it, first securing the letter, which she put in her pocket.

"I hope it will be safe, now," she said, rather contemptuously. "Ain't you ashamed of yourself, Mrs. Mudge?"

"Ashamed of myself!" shrieked that amiable lady, indignant with herself for having quailed for a moment before the old lady.

"What do you mean—you—you pauper?"

"I may be a pauper," said Aunt Lucy, calmly, "But I am thankful to say that I mind my own business, and don't meddle with other people's chests."

A red spot glowed on either cheek of Mrs. Mudge. She was trying hard to find some vantage- ground over the old lady.

"Do you mean to say that I don't mind my business?" she blustered, folding her arms defiantly.

"What were you at my trunk for?" said the old lady, significantly.

"Because it was my duty," was the brazen reply.

Mrs. Mudge had rapidly determined upon her line of defense, and thought it best to carry the war into the enemy's country.

"Yes, I felt sure that your letter was from Paul Prescott, and as he ran away from my husband and me, who were his lawful guardians, it was my duty to take that means of finding out where he is. I knew that you were in league with him, and would do all you could to screen him. This is why I went to your chest, and I would do it again, if necessary."

"Perhaps you have been before," said Aunt Lucy, scornfully. "I think I understand, now, why you were unwilling to give me another key. Fortunately there has been nothing there until now to reward your search."

"You impudent trollop!" shrieked Mrs. Mudge, furiously.

Her anger was the greater, because Aunt Lucy was entirely correct in her supposition that this was not the first visit her landlady had made to the little green chest.

"I'll give Paul the worst whipping he ever had, when I get him back," said Mrs. Mudge, angrily.

"He is beyond your reach, thank Providence," said Aunt Lucy, whose equanimity was not disturbed by this menace, which she knew to be an idle one. "That is enough for you to know. I will take care that you never have another chance to see this letter. And if you ever go to my chest again"—

"Well, ma'am, what then?"

"I shall appeal for protection to 'Squire Newcome."

"Hoity, toity," said Mrs. Mudge, but she was a little alarmed, nevertheless, as such an appeal would probably be prejudicial to her interest.

So from time to time Aunt Lucy received, through Ben, letters from Paul, which kept her acquainted with his progress at school. These letters were very precious to the old lady, and she read them over many times. They formed a bright link of interest which bound her to the outside world, and enabled her to bear up with greater cheerfulness against the tyranny of Mrs. Mudge.

XX.

PAUL OBTAINS A SITUATION.

The month after Paul Prescott succeeded in reaching the head of his class, George Dawkins exerted himself to rise above him. He studied better than usual, and proved in truth a formidable rival. But Paul's spirit was roused. He resolved to maintain his position if possible. He had now become accustomed to study, and it cost him less effort. When the end of the month came, there was considerable speculation in the minds of the boys as to the result of the rivalry. The majority had faith in Paul, but there were some who, remembering how long Dawkins had been at the head of the class, thought he would easily regain his lost rank.

The eventful day, the first of the month, at length came, and the class-list was read.

Paul Prescott ranked first.

George Dawkins ranked second.

A flush spread over the pale face of Dawkins, and he darted a malignant glance at Paul, who was naturally pleased at having retained his rank.

Dawkins had his satellites. One of these came to him at recess, and expressed his regret that Dawkins had failed of success.

Dawkins repelled the sympathy with cold disdain.

"What do you suppose I care for the head of the class?" he demanded, haughtily.

"I thought you had been studying for it."

"Then you thought wrong. Let the sexton's son have it, if he wants it. It would be of no use to me, as I leave this school at the end of the week."

"Leave school!"

The boys gathered about Dawkins, curiously.

"Is it really so, Dawkins?" they inquired.

"Yes," said Dawkins, with an air of importance; "I shall go to a private school, where the advantages are greater than here. My father does not wish me to attend a public school any longer.

This statement was made on the spur of the moment, to cover the mortification which his defeat had occasioned him. It proved true, however. On his return home, Dawkins succeeded in persuading his father to transfer him to a private school, and he took away his books at the end of the week. Had he recovered his lost rank there is no doubt that he would have remained.

Truth to tell, there were few who mourned much for the departure of George Dawkins. He had never been a favorite. His imperious temper and arrogance rendered this impossible.

After he left school, Paul saw little of him for two or three years. At their first encounter Paul bowed and spoke pleasantly, but Dawkins looked superciliously at him without appearing to know him.

Paul's face flushed proudly, and afterwards he abstained from making advances which were likely to be repulsed. He had too much self-respect to submit voluntarily to such slights.

Meanwhile Paul's school life fled rapidly. It was a happy time,—happy in its freedom from care, and happy for him, though all school boys do not appreciate that consideration, in the opportunities for improvement which it afforded. These opportunities, it is only just to Paul to say, were fully improved. He left school with an enviable reputation, and with the good wishes of his schoolmates and teachers.

Paul was now sixteen years old, a stout, handsome boy, with a frank, open countenance, and a general air of health which formed quite a contrast to the appearance he presented when he left the hospitable mansion which Mr. Nicholas
Mudge kept open at the public expense.

Paul was now very desirous of procuring a situation. He felt that it was time he
was doing something for himself. He was ambitious to relieve the kind sexton
and his wife of some portion, at least, of the burden of his support.

Besides, there was the legacy of debt which his father had bequeathed him. Never
for a moment had Paul forgotten it. Never for a moment had he faltered in his
determination to liquidate it at whatever sacrifice to himself.

"My father's name shall be cleared," he said to himself, proudly. "Neither Squire
Conant nor any one else shall have it in his power to cast reproach upon his memory."

The sexton applauded his purpose.

"You are quite right, Paul," he said. "But you need not feel in haste. Obtain your
education first, and the money will come by-and- by. As long as you repay the
amount, principal and interest, you will have done all that you are in honor
bound to do. Squire Conant, as I understand from you, is a rich man, so that he
will experience no hardship in waiting."

Paul was now solicitous about a place. The sexton had little influence, so that he
must depend mainly upon his own inquiries.

He went into the reading-room of the Astor House every day to look over the
advertised wants in the daily papers. Every day he noted down some addresses,
and presented himself as an applicant for a position. Generally, however, he
found that some one else had been before him.

One day his attention was drawn to the following advertisement.

"WANTED. A smart, active, wide-awake boy, of sixteen or seventeen, in a retail
dry- goods store. Apply immediately at—Broadway."

Paul walked up to the address mentioned. Over the door he read, "Smith &
Thompson." This, then, was the firm that had advertised.

The store ran back some distance. There appeared to be six or eight clerks in attendance upon quite a respectable number of customers.

"Is Mr. Smith in?" inquired Paul, of the nearest clerk.

"You'll find him at the lower end of the store. How many yards, ma'am?"

This last was of course addressed to a customer.

Paul made his way, as directed, to the lower end of the store.

A short, wiry, nervous man was writing at a desk.

"Is Mr. Smith in?" asked Paul.

"My name; what can I do for you?" said the short man, crisply.

"I saw an advertisement in the Tribune for a boy."

"And you have applied for the situation?" said Mr. Smith.

"Yes, sir."

"How old are you?" with a rapid glance at our hero.

"Sixteen—nearly seventeen."

"I suppose that means that you will be seventeen in eleven months and a half."

"No, sir," said Paul, "I shall be seventeen in three months."

"All right. Most boys call themselves a year older. What's your name?"

"Paul Prescott."

"P. P. Any relation to Fanny Fern?"

"No, sir," said Paul, rather astonished.

"Didn't know but you might be. P. P. and F. F. Where do you live?"

Paul mentioned the street and number.

"That's well, you are near by," said Mr. Smith. "Now, are you afraid of work?"

"No sir," said Paul, smiling, "not much."

"Well, that's important; how much wages do you expect?"

"I suppose," said Paul, hesitating, "I couldn't expect very much at first."

"Of course not; green, you know. What do you say to a dollar a week?"

"A dollar a week!" exclaimed Paul, in dismay, "I hoped to get enough to pay for my board."

"Nonsense. There are plenty of boys glad enough to come for a dollar a week. At first, you know. But I'll stretch a point with you, and offer you a dollar and a quarter. What do you say?"

"How soon could I expect to have my wages advanced?" inquired our hero, with considerable anxiety.

"Well," said Smith, "at the end of a month or two."

"I'll go home and speak to my uncle about it," said Paul, feeling undecided.

"Can't keep the place open for you. Ah, there's another boy at the door."

"I'll accept," said Paul, jumping to a decision. He had applied in so many different quarters without success, that he could not make up his mind to throw away this chance, poor as it seemed.

"When shall I come?"

"Come to-morrow"

"At what time, sir?"

"At seven o'clock."

This seemed rather early. However, Paul was prepared to expect some discomforts, and signified that he would come.

As he turned to go away, another boy passed him, probably bent on the same errand with himself.

Paul hardly knew whether to feel glad or sorry. He had expected at least three dollars a week, and the descent to a dollar and a quarter was rather disheartening. Still, he was encouraged by the promise of a rise at the end of a month or two,— so on the whole he went home cheerful.

"Well, Paul, what luck to-day?" asked Mr. Cameron, who had just got home as Paul entered.

"I've got a place, Uncle Hugh."

"You have,—where?"

"With Smith & Thompson, No.—Broadway."

"What sort of a store? I don't remember the name."

"It is a retail dry-goods store."

"Did you like the looks of your future employer?"

"I don't know," said Paul, hesitating, "He looked as if he might be a pretty sharp man in business, but I have seen others that I would rather work for. However, beggars mustn't be choosers. But there was one thing I was disappointed about."

"What was that, Paul?"

"About the wages."

"How much will they give you?"

"Only a dollar and a quarter a week, at first."

"That is small, to be sure."

"The most I think of, Uncle Hugh, is, that I shall still be an expense to you. I hoped to get enough to be able to pay my board from the first."

"My dear boy," said the sexton, kindly, "don't trouble yourself on that score. It costs little more for three than for two, and the little I expend on your account is richly made up by the satisfaction we feel in your society, and your good conduct."

"You say that to encourage me, Uncle Hugh," said Paul. "You have done all for me. I have done nothing for you."

"No, Paul, I spoke the truth. Hester and I have both been happier since you came to us. We hope you will long remain with us. You are already as dear to us as the son that we lost."

"Thank you, Uncle Hugh," said Paul, in a voice tremulous with feeling. "I will do all I can to deserve your kindness."

XXI.

SMITH AND THOMPSON'S YOUNG MAN.

At seven o'clock the next morning Paul stood before Smith & Thompson's store.

As he came up on one side, another boy came down on the other, and crossed the street.

"Are you the new boy?" he asked, surveying Paul attentively.

"I suppose so," said Paul. "I've engaged to work for Smith & Thompson."

"All right. I'm glad to see you," said the other.

This looked kind, and Paul thanked him for his welcome.

"O." said the other, bursting into a laugh, "you needn't trouble yourself about thanking me. I'm glad you've come, because now I shan't have to open the store and sweep out. Just lend a hand there; I'll help you about taking down the shutters this morning, and to-morrow you'll have to get along alone."

The two boys opened the store.

"What's your name?" asked Paul's new acquaintance.

"Paul Prescott. What is yours?"

"Nicholas Benton. You may call me MR. Benton."

"Mr. Benton?" repeated Paul in some astonishment.

"Yes; I'm a young man now. I've been Smith & Thompson's boy till now. Now I'm promoted."

Paul looked at MR. Benton with some amusement. That young man was somewhat shorter than himself, and sole proprietor of a stock of pale yellow hair which required an abundant stock of bear's grease to keep it in order. His face was freckled and expressionless. His eyebrows and eyelashes were of the same faded color. He was dressed, however, with some pretensions to smartness. He wore a blue necktie, of large dimensions, fastened by an enormous breast-pin, which, in its already tarnished splendor, suggested strong doubts as to the apparent gold being genuine.

"There's the broom, Paul," said Mr. Benton, assuming a graceful position on the counter.

"You'll have to sweep out; only look sharp about raising a dust, or Smith'll be into your wool."

"What sort of a man is Mr. Smith?" asked Paul, with some curiosity.

"O, he's an out and outer. Sharp as a steel trap. He'll make you toe the mark."

"Do you like him?" asked Paul, not quite sure whether he understood his employer's character from the description.

"I don't like him well enough to advise any of my folks to trade with him," said Mr. Benton.

"Why not?"

"He'd cheat 'em out of their eye teeth if they happened to have any," said the young man coolly, beginning to pick his teeth with a knife.

Paul began to doubt whether he should like Mr. Smith.

"I say," said Mr. Benton after a pause, "have you begun to shave yet?"

Paul looked up to see if his companion were in earnest.

"No," said he; "I haven't got along as far as that. Have you?"

"I," repeated the young man, a little contemptuously, "of course I have. I've shaved for a year and a half."

"Do you find it hard shaving?" asked Paul, a little slyly.

"Well, my beard is rather stiff," said the late BOY, with an important air, "but I've got used to it."

"Ain't you rather young to shave, Nicholas?" asked Paul.

"Mr. Benton, if you please."

"I mean, Mr. Benton."

"Perhaps I was when I begun. But now I am nineteen."

"Nineteen?"

"Yes, that is to say, I'm within a few months of being nineteen. What do you think of my moustache?"

"I hadn't noticed it."

"The store's rather dark," muttered Mr. Benton, who seemed a little annoyed by this answer. "If you'll come a little nearer you can see it."

Drawing near, Paul, after some trouble, descried a few scattering hairs.

"Yes," said he, wanting to laugh, "I see it."

"Coming on finely, isn't it?" asked Mr. Nicholas Benton, complacently.

"Yes," said Paul, rather doubtfully.

"I don't mind letting you into a secret," said Benton, affably, "if you won't mention it. I've been using some of the six weeks' stuff."

"The what?" asked Paul, opening his eyes.

"Haven't you heard of it?" inquired Benton, a little contemptuously. "Where have you been living all your life? Haven't you seen it advertised,—warranted to produce a full set of whiskers or moustaches upon the smoothest face, etc. I got some a week ago, only a dollar. Five weeks from now you'll see something that'll astonish you."

Paul was not a little amused by his new companion, and would have laughed, but that he feared to offend him.

"You'd better get some," said Mr. Benton. "I'll let you just try mine once, if you want to."

"Thank you," said Paul; "I don't think I want to have a moustache just yet."

"Well, perhaps you're right. Being a boy, perhaps it wouldn't be advisable."

"When does Mr. Smith come in?"

"Not till nine."

"And the other clerks?"

"About eight o'clock. I shan't come till eight, to-morrow morning."

"There's one thing I should like to ask you," said Paul. "Of course you won't answer unless you like."

"Out with it."

"How much does Mr. Smith pay you?"

"Ahem!" said Benton, "what does he pay you?"

"A dollar and a quarter a week."

"He paid me a dollar and a half to begin with."

"Did he? He wanted me to come first at a dollar."

"Just like him. Didn't I tell you he was an out and outer? He'll be sure to take you in if you will let him."

"But," said Paul, anxiously, "he said he'd raise it in a month or two."

"He won't offer to; you'll have to tease him. And then how much'll he raise it? Not more than a quarter. How much do you think I get now?"

"How long have you been here?"

"A year and a half."

"Five dollars a week," guessed Paul.

"Five! he only gives me two and a half. That is, he hasn't been paying me but that. Now, of course, he'll raise, as I've been promoted."

"How much do you expect to get now?"

"Maybe four dollars, and I'm worth ten any day. He's a mean old skinflint, Smith is."

This glimpse at his own prospects did not tend to make Paul feel very comfortable. He could not repress a sigh of disappointment when he thought of this mortifying termination of all his brilliant prospects. He had long nourished the hope of being able to repay the good sexton for his outlay in his behalf, besides discharging the debt which his father had left behind him. Now there seemed to be little prospect of either. He had half a mind to resign his place immediately upon the entrance of Mr. Smith, but two considerations dissuaded him; one, that the sum which he was to receive, though small, would at least buy his clothes, and besides, he was not at all certain of obtaining another situation.

With a sigh, therefore, he went about his duties.

He had scarcely got the store ready when some of the clerks entered, and the business of the day commenced. At nine Mr. Smith appeared.

"So you're here, Peter," remarked he, as he caught sight of our hero.

"Paul," corrected the owner of that name.

"Well, well, Peter or Paul, don't make much difference. Both were apostles, if I remember right. All ready for work, eh?"

"Yes, sir," said Paul, neither very briskly nor cheerfully.

"Well," said Mr. Smith, after a pause, "I guess I'll put you into the calico department. Williams, you may take him under your wing. And now Peter,—all the same, Paul,—I've got a word or two to say to you, as I always do to every boy who comes into my store. Don't forget what you're here for? It's to sell goods. Take care to sell something to every man, woman, and child, that comes in your way. That's the way to do business. Follow it up, and you'll be a rich man some day."

"But suppose they don't want anything?" said Paul.

"Make 'em want something," returned Smith, "Don't let 'em off without buying. That's my motto. However, you'll learn."

Smith bustled off, and began in his nervous way to exercise a general supervision over all that was going on in the store. He seemed to be all eyes. While apparently entirely occupied in waiting upon a customer, he took notice of all the customers in the store, and could tell what they bought, and how much they paid.

Paul listened attentively to the clerk under whom he was placed for instruction.

"What's the price of this calico?" inquired a common-looking woman.

"A shilling a yard, ma'am," (this was not in war times.)

"It looks rather coarse."

"Coarse, ma'am! What can you be thinking of? It is a superfine piece of goods. We sell more of it than of any other figure. The mayor's wife was in here yesterday, and bought two dress patterns off of it."

"Did she?" asked the woman, who appeared favorably impressed by this circumstance.

"Yes, and she promised to send her friends here after some of it. You'd better take it while you can get it."

"Will it wash?"

"To be sure it will."

"Then I guess you may cut me off ten yards." This was quickly done, and the woman departed with her purchase.

Five minutes later, another woman entered with a bundle of the same figured calico.

Seeing her coming, Williams hastily slipped the remnant of the piece out of sight.

"I got this calico here," said the newcomer, "one day last week. You warranted it to wash, but I find it won't. Here's a piece I've tried."

She showed a pattern, which had a faded look.

"You've come to the wrong store," said Williams, coolly. "You must have got the calico somewhere else."

"No, I'm sure I got it here. I remember particularly buying it of you."

"You've got a better memory than I have, then. We haven't got a piece of calico like that in the store."

Paul listened to this assertion with unutterable surprise.

"I am quite certain I bought it here," said the woman, perplexed.

"Must have been the next store,—Blake & Hastings. Better go over there."

The woman went out.

"That's the way to do business," said Williams, winking at Paul.

Paul said nothing, but he felt more than ever doubtful about retaining his place.

XXII.

MR. BENTON'S ADVENTURE.

One evening, about a fortnight after his entrance into Smith & Thompson's employment, Paul was putting up the shutters, the business of the day being over. It devolved upon him to open and close the store, and usually he was the last one to go home.

This evening, however, Mr. Nicholas Benton graciously remained behind and assisted Paul in closing the store. This was unusual, and surprised Paul a little. It was soon explained, however.

"Good-night, Nicholas,—I mean, Mr. Benton," said Paul.

"Not quite yet. I want you to walk a little way with me this evening."

Paul hesitated.

"Come, no backing out. I want to confide to you a very important secret."

He looked so mysterious that Paul's curiosity was aroused, and reflecting that it was yet early, he took his companion's proffered arm, and sauntered along by his side.

"What's the secret?" he asked at length, perceiving that Nicholas was silent.

"Wait till we get to a more retired place."

He turned out of Broadway into a side street, where the passers were less numerous.

"I don't think you could guess," said the young man, turning towards our hero.

"I don't think I could."

"And yet," continued Benton, meditatively, "it is possible that you may have noticed something in my appearance just a little unusual, within the last week. Haven't you, now?"

Paul could not say that he had.

Mr. Benton looked a little disappointed.

"Nobody can tell what has been the state of my feelings," he resumed after a pause.

"You ain't sick?" questioned Paul, hastily.

"Nothing of the sort, only my appetite has been a good deal affected. I don't think I have eaten as much in a week as you would in a day," he added, complacently.

"If I felt that way I should think I was going to be sick," said Paul.

"I'll let you into the secret," said Mr. Benton, lowering his voice, and looking carefully about him, to make sure that no one was within hearing distance—"I'M IN LOVE."

This seemed so utterly ludicrous to Paul, that he came very near losing Mr. Benton's friendship forever by bursting into a hearty laugh.

"I didn't think of that," he said.

"It's taken away my appetite, and I haven't been able to sleep nights," continued Mr. Benton, in a cheerful tone. "I feel just as Howard Courtenay did in the great story that's coming out in the Weekly Budget. You've read it, haven't you?"

"I don't think I have," said Paul.

"Then you ought to. It's tiptop. It's rather curious too that the lady looks just as Miranda does, in the same story."

"How is that?"

"Wait a minute, and I'll read the description."

Mr. Benton pulled a paper from his pocket, —the last copy of the Weekly Budget,—and by the light of a street lamp read the following extract to his amused auditor.

"Miranda was just eighteen. Her form was queenly and majestic. Tall and state-ly, she moved among her handmaidens with a dignity which revealed her superi-or rank. Her eyes were dark as night. Her luxuriant tresses,— there, the rest is torn off," said Mr. Benton, in a tone of vexation.

"She is tall, then?" said Paul.

"Yes, just like Miranda."

"Then," said our hero, in some hesitation, "I should think she would not be very well suited to you."

"Why not?" asked Mr. Benton, quickly.

"Because," said Paul, "you're rather short, you know."

"I'm about the medium height," said Mr. Benton, raising himself upon his toes as he spoke.

"Not quite," said Paul, trying not to laugh.

"I'm as tall as Mr. Smith," resumed Mr. Benton, in a tone which warned Paul that this was a forbidden subject. "But you don't ask me who she is."

"I didn't know as you would be willing to tell."

"I shan't tell any one but you. It's Miss Hawkins,—firm of Hawkins & Brewer. That is, her father belongs to the firm, not she. And Paul," here he clutched our hero's arm convulsively, "I've made a declaration of my love, and—and——"

"Well?"

"She has answered my letter."

"Has she?" asked Paul with some curiosity, "What did she say?"

"She has written me to be under her window this evening."

"Why under her window? why didn't she write you to call?"

"Probably she will, but it's more romantic to say, 'be under my window.'"

"Well, perhaps it is; only you know I don't know much about such things."

"Of course not, Paul," said Mr. Benton; "you're only a boy, you know."

"Are you going to be under her window, Nich,—I mean Mr. Benton?"

"Of course. Do you think I would miss the appointment? No earthly power could prevent my doing it."

"Then I had better leave you," said Paul, making a movement to go.

"No, I want you to accompany me as far as the door. I feel—a little agitated. I suppose everybody does when they are in love," added Mr. Benton, complacently.

"Well," said Paul, "I will see you to the door, but I can't stay, for they will wonder at home what has become of me."

"All right."

"Are we anywhere near the house?"

"Yes, it's only in the next street," said Mr. Benton, "O, Paul, how my heart beats! You can't imagine how I feel!"

Mr. Benton gasped for breath, and looked as if he had swallowed a fish bone, which he had some difficulty in getting down.

"You'll know how to understand my feelings sometime, Paul," said Mr. Benton; "when your time comes, I will remember your service of to-night, and I will stand by you."

Paul inwardly hoped that he should never fall in love, if it was likely to affect him in the same way as his companion, but he thought it best not to say so.

By this time they had come in sight of a three-story brick house, with Benjamin Hawkins on the door-plate.

"That's the house," said Mr. Benton, in an agitated whisper.

"Is it?"

"Yes, and that window on the left-hand side is the window of her chamber."

"How do you know?"

"She told me in the letter."

"And where are you to stand?"

"Just underneath, as the clock strikes nine. It must be about the time."

At that moment the city clock struck nine.

Mr. Benton left Paul, and crossing the street, took up his position beneath the window of his charmer, beginning to sing, in a thin, piping voice, as preconcert-ed between them—
"Ever of thee,
I'm fo-o-ondly dreaming."

The song was destined never to be finished.

From his post in a doorway opposite, Paul saw the window softly open. He could distinguish a tall female figure, doubtless Miss Hawkins herself. She held in her hand a pitcher of water, which she emptied with well- directed aim full upon the small person of her luckless admirer.

The falling column struck upon his beaver, thence spreading on all sides. His carefully starched collar became instantly as limp as a rag, while his coat suffered severely from the shower.

His tuneful accents died away in dismay.

"Ow!" he exclaimed, jumping at least a yard, and involuntarily shaking himself like a dog, "who did that?"

There was no answer save a low, musical laugh from the window above, which was involuntarily echoed by Paul.

"What do you mean by laughing at me?" demanded Mr. Benton, smarting with mortification, as he strode across the street, trying to dry his hat with the help of his handkerchief, "Is this what you call friendship?"

"Excuse me," gasped Paul, "but I really couldn't help it."

"I don't see anything to laugh at," continued Mr. Benton, in a resentful tone; "because I have been subjected to unmanly persecution, you must laugh at me, instead of extending to me the sympathy of a friend."

"I suppose you won't think of her any more," said Paul, recovering himself.

"Think of her!" exclaimed Mr. Benton, "would you have me tear her from my heart, because her mercenary parent chooses to frown upon our love, and follow me with base persecution."

"Her parent!"

"Yes, it was he who threw the water upon me. But it shall not avail," the young man continued, folding his arms, and speaking in a tone of resolution, "bolts and bars shall not keep two loving hearts asunder."

"But it wasn't her father," urged Paul, perceiving that Mr. Benton was under a mistake.

"Who was it, then?"

"It was the young lady herself."

"Who threw the water upon me? It is a base slander."

"But I saw her."

"Saw who?"

"A tall young lady with black hair."

"And was it she who threw the water?" asked Mr. Benton, aghast at this unexpected revelation.

"Yes."

"Then she did it at the command of her proud parent."

Paul did not dispute this, since it seemed to comfort Mr. Benton. It is doubtful, however, whether the young man believed it himself, since he straightway fell into a fit of gloomy abstraction, and made no response when Paul bade him "goodnight."

XXIII.

PAUL LOSES HIS SITUATION AND GAINS A FRIEND.

Paul had a presentiment that he should not long remain in the employ of Smith & Thompson; it was not many weeks before this presentiment was verified.

After having received such instruction as was necessary, the calico department was left in Paul's charge. One day a customer in turning over the patterns shown her took up a piece which Paul knew from complaints made by purchasers would not wash.

"This is pretty," said she, "it is just what I have been looking for. You may cut me off twelve yards."

"Yes, ma'am."

"Wait a minute, though," interposed the lady, "will it wash?"

"I don't think it will," said Paul, frankly, "there have been some complaints made about that."

"Then I shall not want it. Let me see what else you have got."

The customer finally departed, having found nothing to suit her.

No sooner had she left the store than Mr. Smith called Paul.

"Well, did you sell that lady anything?"

"No, sir."

"And why not?" demanded Smith, harshly.

"Because she did not like any of the pieces."

"Wouldn't she have ordered a dress pattern if you had not told her the calico would not wash?"

"Yes, sir, I suppose so," said Paul, preparing for a storm.

"Then why did you tell her?" demanded his employer, angrily.

"Because she asked me."

"Couldn't you have told her that it would wash?"

"That would not have been the truth," said Paul, sturdily.

"You're a mighty conscientious young man," sneered Smith, "You're altogether too pious to succeed in business. I discharge you from my employment."

"Very well, sir," said Paul, his heart sinking, but keeping up a brave exterior, "then I have only to bid you good-morning."

"Good-morning, sir," said his employer with mock deference, "I advise you to study for the ministry, and no longer waste your talents in selling calico."

Paul made no reply, but putting on his cap walked out of the store. It was the middle of the week, and Mr. Smith was, of course, owing him a small sum for his services; but Paul was too proud to ask for his money, which that gentleman did not see fit to volunteer.

"I am sure I have done right," thought Paul. "I had no right to misrepresent the goods to that lady. I wonder what Uncle Hugh will say."

"You did perfectly right," said the sexton, after Paul had related the circumstances of his dismissal. "I wouldn't have had you act differently for twenty situations. I have no doubt you will get a better position elsewhere."

"I hope so," said Paul. "Now that I have lost the situation, Uncle Hugh, I don't mind saying that I never liked it."

Now commenced a search for another place. Day after day Paul went out, and day after day he returned with the same want of success.

"Never mind, Paul," said the sexton encouragingly. "When you do succeed, perhaps you'll get something worth waiting for."

One morning Paul went out feeling that something was going to happen,—he didn't exactly know what,—but he felt somehow that there was to be a change in his luck. He went out, therefore, with more hopefulness than usual; yet, when four o'clock came, and nothing had occurred except failure and disappointment, which unhappily were not at all out of the ordinary course, Paul began to think that he was very foolish to have expected anything.

He was walking listlessly along a narrow street, when, on a sudden, he heard an exclamation of terror, of which, on turning round, he easily discovered the cause.

Two spirited horses, attached to an elegant carriage, had been terrified in some way, and were now running at the top of their speed.

There was no coachman on the box; he had dismounted in order to ring at some door, when the horses started. He was now doing his best to overtake the horses, but in a race between man and horse, it is easy to predict which will have the advantage.

There seemed to be but one person in the carriage. It was a lady,—whose face, pale with terror, could be seen from the carriage window. Her loud cries of alarm no doubt terrified the horses still more, and, by accelerating their speed, tended to make matters worse.

Paul was roused from a train of despondent reflections by seeing the horses coming up the street. He instantly comprehended the whole danger of the lady's situation.

Most boys would have thought of nothing but getting out of the way, and leaving the carriage and its inmate to their fate. What, indeed, could a boy do against a pair of powerful horses, almost beside themselves with fright?"

But our hero, as we have already had occasion to see, was brave and self-possessed, and felt an instant desire to rescue the lady, whose glance of helpless terror, as she leaned her head from the window, he could see. Naturally quickwitted, it flashed upon him that the only way to relieve a horse from one terror, was to bring another to bear upon him.

With scarcely a moment's premeditation, he rushed out into the middle of the street, full in the path of the furious horses, and with his cheeks pale, for he knew his danger, but with determined air, he waved his arms aloft, and cried "Whoa!" at the top of his voice.

The horses saw the sudden movement. They saw the boy standing directly in front of them. They heard the word of command to which they had been used, and by a sudden impulse, relieved from the blind terror which had urged them on, they stopped suddenly, and stood still in the middle of the street, still showing in their quivering limbs the agitation through which they had passed.

Just then the coachman, panting with his hurried running, came up and seized them by the head.

"Youngster," said he, "you're a brave fellow. You've done us a good service to-day. You're a pretty cool hand, you are. I don't know what these foolish horses would have done with the carriage if it had not been for you."

"Let me get out," exclaimed the lady, not yet recovered from her fright.

"I will open the door," said Paul, observing that the coachman was fully occupied in soothing the horses.

He sprang forward, and opening the door of the carriage assisted the lady to descend.

She breathed quickly.

"I have been very much frightened," she said; "and I believe I have been in very great danger. Are you the brave boy who stopped the horses?"

Paul modestly answered in the affirmative.

"And how did you do it? I was so terrified that I was hardly conscious of what was passing, till the horses stopped.

Paul modestly related his agency in the matter.

The lady gazed at his flushed face admiringly.

"How could you have so much courage?" she asked. "You might have been trampled to death under the hoofs of the horses."

"I didn't think of that. I only thought of stopping the horses."

"You are a brave boy. I shudder when I think of your danger and mine. I shall not dare to get into the carriage again this afternoon."

"Allow me to accompany you home?" said Paul, politely.

"Thank you; I will trouble you to go with me as far as Broadway, and then I can get into an omnibus."

She turned and addressed some words to the coachman, directing him to drive home as soon as the horses were quieted, adding that she would trust herself to the escort of the young hero, who had rescued her from the late peril.

"You're a lucky boy," thought John, the coachman. "My mistress is one that never does anything by halves. It won't be for nothing that you have rescued her this afternoon."

As they walked along, the lady, by delicate questioning, succeeded in drawing from our hero his hopes and wishes for the future. Paul, who was of a frank and open nature, found it very natural to tell her all he felt and wished.

"He seems a remarkably fine boy," thought the lady to herself. "I should like to do something for him."

They emerged into Broadway.

"I will detain you a little longer," said the lady; "and perhaps trouble you with a parcel."

"I shall be very glad to take it," said Paul politely.

Appleton's bookstore was close at hand. Into this the lady went, followed by her young companion.

A clerk advanced, and inquired her wishes.

"Will you show me some writing-desks?"

"I am going to purchase a writing-desk for a young friend of mine," she explained to Paul; "as he is a boy, like yourself, perhaps you can guide me in the selection."

"Certainly," said Paul, unsuspiciously.

Several desks were shown. Paul expressed himself admiringly of one made of rose-wood inlaid with pearl.

"I think I will take it," said the lady.

The price was paid, and the desk was wrapped up.

"Now," said Mrs. Danforth, for this proved to be her name, "I will trouble you, Paul, to take the desk for me, and accompany me in the omnibus, that is, if you have no other occupation for your time."

"I am quite at leisure," said Paul. "I shall be most happy to do so."

Paul left the lady at the door of her residence in Fifth Avenue, and promised to call on his new friend the next day.

He went home feeling that, though he had met with no success in obtaining a place, he had been very fortunate in rendering so important a service to a lady whose friendship might be of essential service to him.

XXIV.

PAUL CALLS ON MRS. DANFORTH.

"Mrs. Edward Danforth," repeated the sexton, on hearing the story of Paul's exploit.

"Why, she attends our church."

"Do you know Mr. Danforth?" asked Paul, with interest.

"Only by sight. I know him by reputation, however."

"I suppose he is very rich."

"Yes, I should judge so. At any rate, he is doing an extensive business."

"What is his business?"

"He is a merchant."

"A merchant," thought Paul; "that is just what I should like to be, but I don't see much prospect of it."

"How do you like Mrs. Danforth?" inquired the sexton.

"Very much," said Paul, warmly. "She was very kind, and made me feel quite at home in her company."

"I hope she may be disposed to assist you. She can easily do so, in her position."

The next day Paul did not as usual go out in search of a situation. His mind was occupied with thoughts of his coming interview with Mrs. Danforth, and he thought he would defer his business plans till the succeeding day.

At an early hour in the evening, he paused before an imposing residence on Fifth Avenue, which he had seen but not entered the day previous.

He mounted the steps and pulled the bell.

A smart-looking man-servant answered his ring.

"Is Mrs. Danforth at home?" asked Paul.

"Yes, I believe so."

"I have called to see her."

"Does she expect you?" asked the servant, looking surprised.

"Yes; I come at her appointment," said Paul.

"Then I suppose it's all right," said the man. "Will you come in?" he asked, a little doubtfully.

Paul followed him into the house, and was shown into the drawing-room, the magnificence of which somewhat dazzled his eyes; accustomed only to the plain sitting-room of Mr. Cameron.

The servant reappeared after a brief absence, and with rather more politeness than he had before shown, invited Paul to follow him to a private sitting-room upstairs, where he would see Mrs. Danforth.

Looking at Paul's plain, though neat clothes, the servant was a little puzzled to understand what had obtained for Paul the honor of being on visiting terms with Mrs. Danforth.

"Good evening, Paul," said Mrs. Danforth, rising from her seat and welcoming our hero with extended hand. "So you did not forget your appointment."

"There was no fear of that," said Paul, with his usual frankness. "I have been looking forward to coming all day."

"Have you, indeed?" said the lady with a pleasant smile.

"Then I must endeavor to make your visit agreeable to you. Do you recognize this desk?"

Upon a table close by, was the desk which had been purchased the day previous, at Appleton's.

"Yes," said Paul, "it is the one you bought yesterday. I think it is very handsome."

"I am glad you think so. I think I told you that I intended it for a present. I have had the new owner's name engraved upon it."

Paul read the name upon the plate provided for the purpose. His face flushed with surprise and pleasure. That name was his own.

"Do you really mean it for me" he asked.

"If you will accept it," said Mrs. Danforth, smiling.

"I shall value it very much," said Paul, gratefully. "And I feel very much indebted to your kindness."

"We won't talk of indebtedness, for you remember mine is much the greater. If you will open the desk you will find that it is furnished with what will, I hope, prove of use to you."

The desk being opened, proved to contain a liberal supply of stationery, sealing wax, postage stamps, and pens.

Paul was delighted with his new present, and Mrs. Danforth seemed to enjoy the evident gratification with which it inspired him.

"Now," said she, "tell me a little about yourself. Have you always lived in New York?"

"Only about three years," said Paul.

"And where did you live before?"

"At Wrenville, in Connecticut."

"I have heard of the place. A small country town, is it not?" .

Paul answered in the affirmative.

"How did you happen to leave Wrenville, and come to New York?"

Paul blushed, and hesitated a moment.

"I ran away," he said at length, determined to keep nothing back.

"Ran away! Not from home, I hope."

"I had no home," said Paul, soberly. "I should never have left there, if my father had not died. Then I was thrown upon the world. I was sent to the Poorhouse. I did not want to go, for I thought I could support myself."

"That is a very honorable feeling. I suppose you did not fare very well at the Poorhouse."

In reply, Paul detailed some of the grievances to which he had been subjected. Mrs. Danforth listened with sympathizing attention.

"You were entirely justified in running away," she said, as he concluded. "I can hardly imagine so great a lack of humanity as these people showed. You are now, I hope, pleasantly situated?"

"Yes," said Paul, "Mr. and Mrs. Cameron treat me with as great kindness as if I were their own child."

"Cameron! Is not that the name of the sexton of our church?" said Mrs. Danforth, meditatively.

"It is with him that I have a pleasant home."

"Indeed, I am glad to hear it. You have been attending school, I suppose."

"Yes, it is not more than two months since I left off school."

"And now I suppose you are thinking of entering upon some business."

"Yes; I have been trying to obtain a place in some merchant's counting-room."

"You think, then, that you would like the career of a merchant?"

"There is nothing that would suit me better."

"You have not succeeded in obtaining a place yet, I suppose?"

"No. They are very difficult to get, and I have no influential friends to assist me."

"I have heard Mr. Danforth say that he experienced equal difficulty when he came to New York, a poor boy."

Paul looked surprised.

"I see that you are surprised," said Mrs. Danforth, smiling. "You think, perhaps, judging from what you see, that my husband was always rich. But he was the son of a poor farmer, and was obliged to make his own way in the world. By the blessing of God, he has been prospered in business and become rich. But he often speaks of his early discouragements and small beginnings. I am sorry he is not here this evening. By the way, he left word for you to call at his counting-room to- morrow, at eleven o'clock. I will give you his address."

She handed Paul a card containing the specified number, and soon after he withdrew, bearing with him his handsome gift, and a cordial invitation to repeat his call.

He looked back at the elegant mansion which he had just left, and could not help feeling surprised that the owner of such a palace, should have started in life with no greater advantages than himself.

XXV.

AN OLD ACQUAINTANCE.

Paul slept late the next morning. He did not hear the breakfast-bell, and when the sexton came up to awaken him he rubbed his eyes with such an expression of bewilderment that Mr. Cameron could not forbear laughing.

"You must have had queer dreams, Paul," said he.

"Yes, Uncle Hugh," said Paul, laughing, "I believe I have."

"When you have collected your wits, which at present seem absent on a wool-gathering expedition, perhaps you will tell what you have been dreaming about."

"So I will," said Paul, "and perhaps you can interpret it for me. I dreamed that I was back again at Mr. Mudge's, and that he sent me out into the field to dig potatoes. I worked away at the first hill, but found no potatoes. In place of them were several gold pieces. I picked them up in great surprise, and instead of putting them into the basket, concluded to put them in my pocket. But as all the hills turned out in the same way I got my pockets full, and had to put the rest in the basket. I was just wondering what they would do for potatoes, when all at once a great dog came up and seized me by the arm——"

"And you opened your eyes and saw me," said the sexton, finishing out his narrative.

"Upon my word, that's very complimentary to me. However, some of our potatoes have escaped transformation into gold pieces, but I am afraid you will find them rather cold if you don't get down to breakfast pretty quick."

"All right, Uncle Hugh. I'll be down in a jiffy."

About half-past ten Paul started on his way to Mr. Danforth's counting-room. It was located on Wall Street, as he learned from the card which had been given him by Mrs. Danforth. He felt a little awkward in making this call. It seemed as if he were going to receive thanks for the service which he had rendered, and he felt that he had already been abundantly repaid. However, he was bound in courtesy to call, since he did so at the request of Mrs. Danforth.

It was a large stone building, divided up into offices, to which Paul had been directed. Mr. Danforth's office he found after a little search, upon the second floor.

He opened the door with a little embarrassment, and looked about him.

In one corner was a small room, used as a more private office, the door of which was closed. In the larger room the only one whom he saw, was a boy, apparently about his own age, who was standing at a desk and writing.

This boy looked around as Paul entered, and he at once recognized in him an old acquaintance.

"George Dawkins!" he exclaimed in surprise.

The latter answered in a careless indifferent tone, not exhibiting any very decided pleasure at meeting his old schoolmate.

"Oh, it's you, Prescott, is it?"

"Yes," said Paul, "I haven't met you since you left our school."

"No, I believe we have not met," said Dawkins, in the same tone as before.

"How long have you been in this office?" asked our hero.

"I really can't say," said Dawkins, not looking up.

"You can't say!"

"No, I'm rather forgetful."

Paul could not help feeling chilled at the indifferent manner in which his advances were met. He had been really glad to see Dawkins, and had addressed him with cordiality. He could not conceal from himself that Dawkins did not seem inclined to respond to it.

"Still," thought Paul, extenuatingly, "perhaps that is his way."

As the conversation began to flag, Paul was reminded of his errand by Dawkins saying, in a tone which was half a sneer, "Have you any business with Mr. Danforth this morning, or did you merely come in out of curiosity?"

"I have called to see Mr. Danforth," said Paul.

"He is usually pretty busy in the morning," said Dawkins.

"He directed me to call in the morning," said Paul, sturdily.

"Oh, indeed!" said Dawkins, a little surprised. "I wonder," he thought, "what business this fellow can have with Mr. Danforth. Can he be fishing for a place?"

"Mr. Danforth is engaged with a visitor just now," he at length condescended to say; "if your time is not too valuable to wait, you can see him by-and-by."

"Thank you," said Paul, rather nettled, "you are very polite."

To this Dawkins made no reply, but resumed his pen, and for the next ten minutes seemed entirely oblivious of Paul's presence.

Our hero took up the morning paper, and began, as he had so often done before, to look over the list of wants, thinking it possible he might find some opening for himself.

About ten minutes later the door of the inner office opened, and two gentlemen came out. One was a gentleman of fifty, a business friend of Mr. Danforth's, the other was Mr. Danforth himself.

The former remarked, on seeing Paul, "Is this your son, Danforth?"

"No," said the merchant, nodding in a friendly manner to Paul.

"That's a good joke," thought Dawkins, chuckling to himself; "Mr. Danforth must be immensely flattered at having a sexton's adopted son taken for his."

After a final word or two on business matters, and arrangements for another interview, the visitor departed, and Mr. Danforth, now at leisure, turned to Paul.

"Now my lad," he said kindly, "if you will follow me, we shall have a chance to talk a little."

Paul followed the merchant into his office, the door of which was closed, much to the regret of Dawkins, who had a tolerably large share of curiosity, and was very anxious to find out what business Paul could possibly have with his employer.

"Take that seat, if you please;" said Mr. Danforth, motioning Paul to an armchair, and sitting down himself, "Mrs. Danforth told me from how great a peril you rescued her. You are a brave boy."

"I don't know," said Paul, modestly, "I didn't think of the danger. If I had, perhaps I should have hesitated."

"If you had not been brave you would have thought of your own risk. My wife and myself are under very great obligations to you."

"That more than repays me for all I did," said Paul, in a tone of mingled modesty and manliness.

"I like the boy," thought Mr. Danforth; "he is certainly quite superior to the common run."

"Have you left school?" he inquired, after a pause.

"Yes, sir. Last term closed my school life."

"Then you have never been in a situation."

"Yes, sir."

"Indeed! Before you left school?"

"No, sir, since."

"You did not like it, then?"

"No, sir," said Paul.

"And was that the reason of your leaving?"

"No, sir; my employer was not satisfied with me," said Paul, frankly.

"Indeed! I am surprised to hear this! If you have no objection, will you tell me the circumstances?"

Paul related in a straightforward manner the difficulty he had had with Smith & Thompson.

"I hope you don't think I did wrong," he concluded.

"By no means," said Mr. Danforth, warmly. "Your conduct was entirely cred-itable. As for Smith, I know of him. He is a sharper. It would have done you no good to remain in his employ."

Paul was pleased with this commendation. He had thought it possible that his dismissal from his former situation might operate against him with the merchant.

"What are your present plans and wishes?" asked Mr. Danforth, after a slight pause.

"I should like to enter a merchant's counting-room," said Paul, "but as such places are hard to get, I think I shall try to get into a store."

Mr. Danforth reflected a moment, then placing a piece of paper before our hero, he said, "Will you write your name and address on this piece of paper, that I may know where to find you, in case I hear of a place?"

Paul did as directed. He had an excellent handwriting, a point on which the mer-chant set a high value.

The latter surveyed the address with approval, and said, "I am glad you write so excellent a hand. It will be of material assistance to you in securing a place in a counting- room. Indeed, it has been already, for I have just thought of a place which I can obtain for you."

"Can you, sir?" said Paul, eagerly.

"Where is it?"

"In my own counting-room," said Mr. Danforth, smiling.

"I am very much obliged to you," said Paul, hardly believing his ears.

"I was prepared to give it to you when you came in, in case I found you qualified. The superiority of your handwriting decides me. When can you come?"

"To-morrow, if you like, sir."

"I like your promptness. As it is the middle of the week, however, you may take a vacation till Monday. Your salary will begin to-morrow."

"Thank you, sir."

"I will give you five dollars per week at first, and more as your services become more valuable. Will that be satisfactory?"

"I shall feel rich, sir. Mr. Smith only gave me a dollar and a quarter."

"I hope you will find other differences between me and Mr. Smith," said the merchant, smiling.

These preliminaries over, Mr. Danforth opened the door, and glancing at Dawkins, said, "Dawkins, I wish you to become acquainted with your fellow clerk, Paul Prescott."

Dawkins looked surprised, and anything but gratified as he responded stiffly, "I have the honor of being already acquainted with Mr. Prescott."

"He is a little jealous of an interloper," thought Mr. Danforth, noticing the repellent manner of young Dawkins. "Never mind, they will get acquainted after awhile."

When George Dawkins went home to dinner, his father observed the dissatisfied look he wore.

"Is anything amiss, my son?" he inquired.

"I should think there was," grumbled his son.

"What is it?"

"We've got a new clerk, and who do you think it is?"

"Who is it?"

"The adopted son of old Cameron, the sexton."

"Indeed," said Mrs. Dawkins. "I really wonder at Mr. Danforth's bad taste. There are many boys of genteel family, who would have been glad of the chance. This boy is a low fellow of course."

"Certainly," said her son, though he was quite aware that this was not true.

"What could have brought the boy to Danforth's notice?" asked Dawkins, senior.

"I don't know, I'm sure. The boy has managed to get round him in some way. He is very artful."

"I really think, husband, that you ought to remonstrate with Mr. Danforth about taking such a low fellow into his counting-room with our George."

"Pooh!" said Mr. Dawkins, who was a shade more sensible than his wife, "he'd think me a meddler."

"At any rate, George," pursued his mother, "there's one thing that is due to your family and bringing up,—not to associate with this low fellow any more than business requires."

"I certainly shall not," said George, promptly.

He was the worthy son of such a mother.

XXVI.

A VULGAR RELATION.

At the end of the first week, Paul received five dollars, the sum which the merchant had agreed to pay him for his services. With this he felt very rich. He hurried home, and displayed to the sexton the crisp bank note which had been given him.

"You will soon be a rich man, Paul," said Mr. Cameron, with a benevolent smile, returning the bill.

"But I want you to keep it, Uncle Hugh."

"Shall I put it in the Savings Bank, for you, Paul?"

"I didn't mean that. You have been supporting me—giving me board and clothes—for three years. It is only right that you should have what I earn."

"The offer is an honorable one on your part, Paul," said the sexton; "but I don't need it. If it will please you, I will take two dollars a week for your board, now, and out of the balance you may clothe yourself, and save what you can."

This arrangement seemed to be a fair one. Mr. Cameron deposited the five dollar note in his pocket-book, and passed one of three dollars to Paul. This sum our hero deposited the next Monday morning, in a savings bank. He estimated that he could clothe himself comfortably for fifty dollars a year. This would leave him one hundred towards the payment of the debt due to Squire Conant.

"By-and-by my salary will be raised," thought Paul. "Then I can save more."

He looked forward with eager anticipation to the time when he should be able to redeem his father's name, and no one would be entitled to cast reproach upon his memory.

He endeavored to perform his duties faithfully in the office, and to learn as rapidly as he could the business upon which he had entered. He soon found that he must depend mainly upon himself. George Dawkins seemed disposed to afford him no assistance, but repelled scornfully the advances which Paul made towards cordiality. He was by no means as faithful as Paul, but whenever Mr. Danforth was absent from the office, spent his time in lounging at the window, or reading a cheap novel, with one of which he was usually provided.

When Paul became satisfied that Dawkins was not inclined to accept his overtures, he ceased to court his acquaintance, and confined himself to his own desk.

One day as he was returning from dinner, he was startled by an unceremonious slap upon the shoulder.

Looking up in some surprise, he found that this greeting had come from a man just behind him, whose good-humored face and small, twinkling eyes, he at once recognized.

"How do you do, Mr. Stubbs?" inquired Paul, his face lighting up with pleasure.

"I'm so's to be round. How be you?" returned the worthy pedler, seizing our hero's hand and shaking it heartily.

Mr. Stubbs was attired in all the glory of a blue coat with brass buttons and swallow tails.

"When did you come to New York?" asked Paul.

"Just arrived; that is, I got in this mornin'. But I say, how you've grown. I shouldn't hardly have known you."

"Shouldn't you, though?" said Paul, gratified as most boys are, on being told that he had grown. "Have you come to the city on business?"

"Well, kinder on business, and kinder not. I thought I'd like to have a vacation. Besides, the old lady wanted a silk dress, and she was sot on havin' it bought in York. So I come to the city."

"Where are you stopping, Mr. Stubbs?"

"Over to the Astor House. Pretty big hotel, ain't it?"

"Yes, I see you are traveling in style."

"Yes, I suppose they charge considerable, but I guess I can stand it. I hain't been drivin' a tin-cart for nothin' the last ten years.

"How have you been enjoying yourself since you arrived?"

"Oh, pretty well. I've been round seeing the lions, and came pretty near seeing the elephant at one of them Peter Funk places."

"You did! Tell me about it."

"You see I was walkin' along when a fellow came out of one of them places, and asked me if I wouldn't go in. I didn't want to refuse such a polite invitation, and besides I had a curiosity to see what there was to be seen, so I went in. They put up a silver watch, I could see that it was a good one, and so I bid on it. It ran up to eight dollars and a quarter. I thought it was a pity it should go off so cheap, so I bid eight and a half."

"'Eight and a half and sold,' said the man; 'shall I put it up for you?"

"'No, I thank you,' said I, 'I'll take it as it is.'

"'But I'll put it up in a nice box for you,' said he.

"I told him I didn't care for the box. He seemed very unwilling to let it go, but I took it out of his hand and he couldn't help himself. Well, when they made out the bill, what do you suppose they charged?"

"I don't know."

"Why, eighteen and a half."

"Look here,' said I, 'I guess here's something of a mistake. You've got ten dollars too much.'

"I think you must be mistaken,' said he, smiling a foxy smile.

"You know I am not,' said I, rather cross.

"We can't let that watch go for any thing shorter,' said he, coolly.

"Just then a man that was present stepped up and said, 'the man is right; don't attempt to impose upon him.'

"With that he calmed right down. It seems it was a policeman who was sent to watch them, that spoke. So I paid the money, but as I went out I heard the auctioneer say that the sale was closed for the day. I afterwards learned that if I had allowed them to put the watch in a box, they would have exchanged it for another that was only plated."

"Do you know anybody in the city?" asked Paul.

"I've got some relations, but I don't know where they live."

"What is the name?" asked Paul, "we can look into the directory."

"The name is Dawkins," answered the pedler.

"Dawkins!" repeated Paul, in surprise.

"Yes, do you happen to know anybody of the name?"

"Yes, but I believe it is a rich family."

"Well, so are my relations," said Jehoshaphat. "You didn't think Jehoshaphat Stubbs had any rich relations, did you? These, as I've heard tell, hold their heads as high as anybody."

"Perhaps I may be mistaken," said Paul.

"What is the name—the Christian name, I mean—of your relation?"

"George."

"It must be he, then. There is a boy of about my own age of that name. He works in the same office."

"You don't say so! Well, that is curious, I declare. To think that I should have happened to hit upon you so by accident too."

"How are you related to them?" inquired Paul.

"Why, you see, I'm own cousin to Mr. Dawkins. His father and my mother were brother and sister."

"What was his father's business?" asked Paul.

"I don't know what his regular business was, but he was a sexton in some church."

This tallied with the account Paul had received from Mr. Cameron, and he could no longer doubt that, strange as it seemed, the wealthy Mr. Dawkins was own cousin to the pedler.

"Didn't you say the boy was in the same office with you, Paul?"

"Yes."

"Well, I've a great mind to go and see him, and find out where his father lives. Perhaps I may get an invite to his house."

"How shocked Dawkins will be!" thought Paul, not, it must be confessed, without a feeling of amusement. He felt no compunction in being the instrument of mortifying the false pride of his fellow clerk, and he accordingly signified to Mr. Stubbs that he was on his way to the counting-room.

"Are you, though? Well, I guess I'll go along with you. Is it far off?"

"Only in the next street."

The pedler, it must be acknowledged, had a thoroughly countrified appearance. He was a genuine specimen of the Yankee,—a long, gaunt figure, somewhat stooping, and with a long aquiline nose. His dress has already been described.

As Dawkins beheld him entering with Paul, he turned up his nose in disgust at what he considered Paul's friend.

What was his consternation when the visitor, approaching him with a benignant smile, extended his brown hand, and said, "How d'ye do, George? How are ye all to hum?"

Dawkins drew back haughtily.

"What do you mean?" he said, pale with passion.

"Mr. Dawkins," said Paul, with suppressed merriment, "allow me to introduce your cousin, Mr. Stubbs."

"Jehoshaphat Stubbs," explained that individual. "Didn't your father never mention my name to you?"

"Sir," said Dawkins, darting a furious glance at Paul, "you are entirely mistaken if you suppose that any relationship exists between me and that—person."

"No, it's you that are mistaken," said Mr. Stubbs, persevering, "My mother was Roxana Jane Dawkins. She was own sister to your grandfather. That makes me and your father cousins Don't you see?"

"I see that you are intending to insult me," said Dawkins, the more furiously, because he began to fear there might be some truth in the man's claims. "Mr. Prescott, I leave you to entertain your company yourself."

And he threw on his hat and dashed out of the counting-room.

"Well," said the pedler, drawing a long breath, "that's cool,—denyin' his own flesh and blood. Rather stuck up, ain't he?"

"He is, somewhat," said Paul; "if I were you, I shouldn't be disposed to own him as a relation."

"Darned ef I will!" said Jehoshaphat sturdily; "I have some pride, ef I am a pedler. Guess I'm as good as he, any day."

XXVII.

MR. MUDGE'S FRIGHT.

Squire Newcome sat in a high-backed chair before the fire with his heels on the fender. He was engaged in solemnly perusing the leading editorial in the evening paper, when all at once the table at his side gave a sudden lurch, the lamp slid into his lap, setting the paper on fire, and, before the Squire realized his situation, the flames singed his whiskers, and made his face unpleasantly warm.

"Cre-a-tion!" he exclaimed, jumping briskly to his feet.

The lamp had gone out, so that the cause of the accident remained involved in mystery. The Squire had little trouble in conjecturing, however, that Ben was at the bottom of it.

Opening the door hastily, he saw, by the light in the next room, that young gentleman rising from his knees in the immediate vicinity of the table.

"Ben-ja-min," said the Squire, sternly,

"What have you been a-doing?"

Ben looked sheepish, but said nothing.

"I repeat, Benjamin, what have you been a-doing?"

"I didn't mean to," said Ben.

"That does not answer my interrogatory. What have you been a-doing?"

"I was chasing the cat," said Ben, "and she got under the table. I went after her, and somehow it upset. Guess my head might have knocked against the legs."

"How old are you, Benjamin?"

"Fifteen."

"A boy of fifteen is too old to play with cats. You may retire to your dormitory."

"It's only seven o'clock, father," said Ben, in dismay.

"Boys that play with cats are young enough to retire at seven," remarked the Squire, sagaciously.

There was nothing for Ben but to obey.

Accordingly with reluctant steps he went up to his chamber and went to bed. His active mind, together with the early hour, prevented his sleeping. Instead, his fertile imagination was employed in devising some new scheme, in which, of course, fun was to be the object attained. While he was thinking, one scheme flashed upon him which he at once pronounced "bully."

"I wish I could do it to-night," he sighed.

"Why can't I?" he thought, after a moment's reflection.

The more he thought of it, the more feasible it seemed, and at length he decided to attempt it.

Rising from his bed he quickly dressed himself, and then carefully took the sheet, and folding it up in small compass put it under his arm.

Next, opening the window, he stepped out upon the sloping roof of the ell part, and slid down to the end where he jumped off, the height not being more than four feet from the ground. By some accident, a tub of suds was standing under the eaves, and Ben, much to his disgust, jumped into it.

"Whew!" exclaimed he, "I've jumped into that plaguy tub. What possessed Hannah to put it in a fellow's way?"

At this moment the back door opened, and Hannah called out, in a shrill voice, "Who's there?" Ben hastily hid himself, and thought it best not to answer.

"I guess 'twas the cat," said Hannah, as she closed the door.

"A two-legged cat," thought Ben, to himself; "thunder, what sopping wet feet I've got. Well, it can't be helped."

With the sheet still under his arm, Ben climbed a fence and running across the fields reached the fork of the road. Here he concealed himself under a hedge, and waited silently till the opportunity for playing his practical joke arrived.

I regret to say that Mr. Mudge, with whom we have already had considerable to do, was not a member of the temperance society. Latterly, influenced perhaps by Mrs. Mudge's tongue, which made his home far from a happy one, he had got into the habit of spending his evenings at the tavern in the village, where he occasionally indulged in potations that were not good for him. Generally, he kept within the bounds of moderation, but occasionally he exceeded these, as he had done on the present occasion.

Some fifteen minutes after Ben had taken his station, he saw, in the moonlight, Mr. Mudge coming up the road, on his way home. Judging from his zigzag course, he was not quite himself.

Ben waited till Mr. Mudge was close at hand, when all at once he started from his place of concealment completely enveloped in the sheet with which he was provided. He stood motionless before the astounded Mudge.

"Who are you?" exclaimed Mudge, his knees knocking together in terror, clinging to an overhanging branch for support.

There was no answer.

"Who are you?" he again asked in affright.

"Sally Baker," returned Ben, in as sepulchral a voice as he could command.

Sally Baker was an old pauper, who had recently died. The name occurred to Ben on the spur of the moment. It was with some difficulty that he succeeded in getting out the name, such was his amusement at Mr. Mudge's evident terror.

"What do you want of me?" inquired Mudge, nervously.

"You half starved me when I was alive," returned Ben, in a hollow voice, "I must be revenged."

So saying he took one step forward, spreading out his arms. This was too much for Mr. Mudge. With a cry he started and ran towards home at the top of his speed, with Ben in pursuit.

"I believe I shall die of laughing, exclaimed Ben, pausing out of breath, and sitting down on a stone, "what a donkey he is, to be sure, to think there are such things as ghosts. I'd like to be by when he tells Mrs. Mudge."

After a moment's thought, Ben wrapped up the sheet, took it under his arm, and once more ran in pursuit of Mr. Mudge.

Meanwhile Mrs. Mudge was sitting in the kitchen of the Poorhouse, mending stockings. She was not in the pleasantest humor, for one of the paupers had managed to break a plate at tea-table (if that can be called tea where no tea is provided), and trifles were sufficient to ruffle Mrs. Mudge's temper.

"Where's Mudge, I wonder?" she said, sharply; "over to the tavern, I s'pose, as usual. There never was such a shiftless, good-for- nothing man. I'd better have stayed unmarried all the days of my life than have married him. If he don't get in by ten, I'll lock the door, and it shall stay locked. 'Twill serve him right to stay out doors all night."

Minutes slipped away, and the decisive hour approached.

"I'll go to the door and look out," thought Mrs. Mudge, "if he ain't anywhere in sight I'll fasten the door."

She laid down her work and went to the door.

She had not quite reached it when it was flung open violently, and Mr. Mudge, with a wild, disordered look, rushed in, nearly over- turning his wife, who gazed at him with mingled anger and astonishment.

"What do you mean by this foolery, Mudge?" she demanded, sternly.

"What do I mean?" repeated her husband, vaguely.

"I needn't ask you," said his wife, contemptuously. "I see how it is, well enough. You're drunk!"

"Drunk!"

"Yes, drunk; as drunk as a beast."

"Well, Mrs. Mudge," hiccoughed her husband, in what he endeavored to make a dignified tone, "you'd be drunk too if you'd seen what I've seen."

"And what have you seen, I should like to know?" said Mrs. Mudge.

Mudge rose with some difficulty, steadied himself on his feet, and approaching his wife, whispered in a tragic tone, "Mrs. Mudge, I've seen a sperrit."

"It's plain enough that you've seen spirit," retorted his wife. "'Tisn't many nights that you don't, for that matter. You ought to be ashamed of yourself, Mudge."

"It isn't that," said her husband, shaking his hand, "it's a sperrit,—a ghost, that I've seen."

"Indeed!" said Mrs. Mudge, sarcastically, "perhaps you can tell whose it is."

"It was the sperrit of Sally Baker," said Mudge, solemnly.

"What did she say?" demanded Mrs. Mudge, a little curiously.

"She said that I—that we, half starved her, and then she started to run after me—and— oh, Lordy, there she is now!"

Mudge jumped trembling to his feet. Following the direction of his outstretched finger, Mrs. Mudge caught a glimpse of a white figure just before the window. I need hardly say that it was Ben, who had just arrived upon the scene.

Mrs. Mudge was at first stupefied by what she saw, but being a woman of courage she speedily recovered herself, and seizing the broom from behind the door, darted out in search of the "spirit." But Ben, perceiving that he was discovered, had disappeared, and there was nothing to be seen.

"Didn't I tell you so?" muttered Mudge, as his wife re-entered, baffled in her attempt, "you'll believe it's a sperrit, now."

"Go to bed, you fool!" retorted his wife.

This was all that passed between Mr. and Mrs. Mudge on the subject. Mr. Mudge firmly believes, to this day, that the figure which appeared to him was the spirit of Sally Baker.

XXVIII.

HOW BEN GOT HOME.

Delighted with the complete success of his practical joke, Ben took his way home-ward with the sheet under his arm. By the time he reached his father's house it was ten o'clock. The question for Ben to consider now was, how to get in. If his father had not fastened the front door he might steal in, and slip up stairs on tip-toe without being heard. This would be the easiest way of overcoming the diffi-culty, and Ben, perceiving that the light was still burning in the sitting-room, had some hopes that he would be able to adopt it. But while he was only a couple of rods distant he saw the lamp taken up by his father, who appeared to be moving from the room.

"He's going to lock the front door," thought Ben, in disappointment; "if I had only got along five minutes sooner."

From his post outside he heard the key turn in the lock.

The 'Squire little dreamed that the son whom he imagined fast asleep in his room was just outside the door he was locking.

"I guess I'll go round to the back part of the house," thought Ben, "perhaps I can get in the same way I came out."

Accordingly he went round and managed to clamber upon the roof, which was only four feet from the ground. But a brief trial served to convince our young adventurer that it is a good deal easier sliding down a roof than it is climbing up. The shingles being old were slippery, and though the ascent was not steep, Ben found the progress he made was very much like that of a man at the bottom of a well, who is reported as falling back two feet for every three that he ascended. What increased the difficulty of his attempt was that the soles of his shoes were well worn, and slippery as well as the shingles.

"I never can get up this way," Ben concluded, after several fruitless attempts; "I know what I'll do," he decided, after a moment's perplexity; "I'll pull off my shoes and stockings, and then I' guess I can get along better."

Ben accordingly got down from the roof, and pulled off his shoes and stockings. As he wanted to carry these with him, he was at first a little puzzled by this new difficulty. He finally tied the shoes together by the strings and hung them round his neck. He disposed of the stockings by stuffing one in each pocket.

"Now," thought Ben, "I guess I can get along better. I don't know what to do with the plaguy sheet, though."

But necessity is the mother of invention, and Ben found that he could throw the sheet over his shoulders, as a lady does with her shawl. Thus accoutered he recommenced the ascent with considerable confidence.

He found that his bare feet clung to the roof more tenaciously than the shoes had done, and success was already within his grasp, when an unforeseen mishap frustrated his plans. He had accomplished about three quarters of the ascent when all at once the string which united the shoes which he had hung round his neck gave way, and both fell with a great thump on the roof. Ben made a clutch for them in which he lost his own hold, and made a hurried descent in their company, alighting with his bare feet on some flinty gravel stones, which he found by no means agreeable.

"Ow!" ejaculated Ben, limping painfully, "them plaguy gravel stones hurt like thunder. I'll move 'em away the first thing to-morrow. If that confounded shoe-string hadn't broken I'd have been in bed by this time."

Meanwhile Hannah had been sitting over the kitchen fire enjoying a social chat with a "cousin" of hers from Ireland, a young man whom she had never seen or heard of three months before. In what way he had succeeded in convincing her of the relationship I have never been able to learn, but he had managed to place himself on familiar visiting terms with the inmate of 'Squire Newcome's kitchen.

"It's only me cousin, sir," Hannah explained to the 'Squire, when he had questioned her on the subject; "he's just from Ireland, sir, and it seems like home to see him."

On the present occasion Tim Flaherty had outstayed his usual time, and was still in the kitchen when Ben reached home. They did not at first hear him, but when he made his last abortive attempt, and the shoes came clattering down, they could not help hearing.

"What's that?" asked Hannah, listening attentively.

She went to the door to look out, her cousin following.

There was nothing to be seen.

"Perhaps you was dramin' Hannah," said Tim, "more by token, it's time we was both doin' that same, so I'll bid you good-night."

"Come again soon, Tim," said Hannah, preparing to close the door.

A new plan of entrance flashed upon Ben.

He quickly put on his shoes and stockings, unfolded the sheet and prepared to enact the part of a ghost once more,—this time for the special benefit of Hannah.

After fully attiring himself he came to the back door which Hannah had already locked, and tapped three times.

Hannah was engaged in raking out the kitchen fire.

"Sure it's Tim come back," thought she, as she went to the door. "Perhaps he's forgotten something."

She opened the door unsuspiciously, fully expecting to see her Irish cousin standing before her.

What was her terror on beholding a white- robed figure, with extended arms.

"Howly virgin, defend me!" she exclaimed, in paralyzing terror, which was increased by a guttural sound which proceeded from the throat of the ghost, who at the same time waved his arms aloft, and made a step towards Hannah.

Hannah, with a wild howl dropped the lamp and fed towards the sitting-room, where 'Squire Newcome was still sitting.

Ben sped upstairs at the top of his speed, dashed into his own chamber, spread the sheet on the bed, and undressed so rapidly that he seemed only to shake his clothes off, and jumped into bed. He closed his eyes and appeared to be in a profound slumber.

Hannah's sudden appearance in the sitting- room in such a state naturally astonished the 'Squire.

"What's the matter?" he demanded of the affrighted servant.

"Oh, sir," she gasped, "I'm almost kilt entirely."

"Are you?" said the 'Squire, "you appear to be more frightened than hurt."

"Yes, sir, shure I am frightened, which indeed I couldn't help it, sir, for I never saw a ghost before in all my life."

"A ghost! What nonsense are you talking, Hannah?"

"Shure it's not nonsense, for it's just now that the ghost came to the door, sir, and knocked, and I went to the door thinking it might be me cousin, who's been passing the evening with me, when I saw a great white ghost, ten foot tall, standing forninst me."

"Ten feet tall?"

"Yes, sir, and he spread out his arms and spoke in a terrible voice, and was going to carry me off wid him, but I dropped the lamp, and O sir, I'm kilt entirely."

"This is a strange story," said 'Squire Newcome, rather suspiciously; "I hope you have not been drinking."

Hannah protested vehemently that not a drop of liquor had passed her lips, which was true.

"I'll go out and hunt for the ghost," said the 'Squire.

"Oh, don't sir. He'll carry you off," said Hannah, terrified.

"Nonsense!" exclaimed the 'Squire. "Follow me, or you may stay here if you are frightened."

This Hannah would by no means do, since the 'Squire had taken the lamp and she would be left in the dark.

Accordingly she followed him with a trembling step, as he penetrated through the kitchen into the back room, ready to run at the least alarm.

The back-door was wide open, but nothing was to be seen of the ghost.

"Perhaps the ghost's up-stairs," said Hannah, "I can't sleep up there this night, shure."

But something had attracted Squire Newcome's attention. It was quite muddy out of doors, and Ben had tracked in considerable mud with him. The footprints were very perceptible on the painted floor.

"The ghost seems to have had muddy shoes," said the 'Squire dryly; "I guess I can find him."

He followed the tracks which witnessed so strongly against Ben, to whose chamber they led.

Ben, though still awake, appeared to be in a profound slumber.

"Ben-ja-min!" said his father, stooping over the bed.

There was no answer.

"Ben-ja-min!" repeated his father, giving him a shake, "what does all this mean?"

"What?" inquired Ben, opening his eyes, and looking very innocent.

"Where have you been, to-night?"

"You sent me to bed," said Ben, "and I came."

But the 'Squire was not to be deceived. He was already in possession of too much information to be put off. So Ben, who with all his love of mischief was a boy of truth, finally owned up everything. His father said very little, but told him the next morning that he had made up his mind to send him to a military boarding-school, where the discipline was very strict. Ben hardly knew whether to he glad or sorry, but finally, as boys like change and variety, came to look upon his new prospects with considerable cheerfulness.

XXIX.

DAWKINS IN DIFFICULTIES.

George Dawkins was standing at his desk one morning, when a man entered the office, and stepping up to him, unceremoniously tapped him on the shoulder.

Dawkins turned. He looked extremely annoyed on perceiving his visitor, whose outward appearance was certainly far from prepossessing. His face exhibited unmistakable marks of dissipation, nor did the huge breast pin and other cheap finery which he wore conceal the fact of his intense vulgarity. His eyes were black and twinkling, his complexion very dark, and his air that of a foreigner. He was, in fact, a Frenchman, though his language would hardly have betrayed him, unless, as sometimes, he chose to interlard his discourse with French phrases.

"How are you this morning, my friend?" said the newcomer.

"What are you here for?" asked Dawkins, roughly.

"That does not seem to me a very polite way of receiving your friends."

"Friends!" retorted Dawkins, scornfully, "who authorized you to call yourself my friend?"

"Creditor, then, if it will suit you better, mon ami."

"Hush," said Dawkins, in an alarmed whisper, "he will hear," here he indicated Paul with his finger.

"And why should I care? I have no secrets from the young man."

"Stop, Duval," exclaimed Dawkins, in an angry whisper, "Leave the office at once. Your appearing here will injure me."

"But I am not your friend; why should I care?" sneered Duval.

"Listen to reason. Leave me now, and I will meet you when and where you will."

"Come, that sounds better."

"Now go. I'm afraid Mr. Danforth will be in."

"If he comes, introduce me."

Dawkins would like to have knocked the fellow over.

"Name your place and time, and be quick about it," said he impatiently.

"Eight o'clock this evening, you know where," was the answer.

"Very well. Good-morning."

"Mind you bring some money."

"Good-morning," returned Dawkins, angrily.

At length, much to his relief, Duval left the office. Dawkins stole a side glance at Paul, to see what impression the interview had made upon him, but our hero, who had overheard some portions of the dialogue, perceiving that Dawkins wished it to be private, took as little notice of the visitor as possible. He could not help thinking, however, that Duval was a man whose acquaintance was likely to be of little benefit to his fellow clerk.

Throughout the day Dawkins appeared unusually nervous, and made several blunders which annoyed Mr. Danforth. Evidently he had something on his mind. Not to keep the reader in suspense, George had fallen among bad companions, where he had learned both to drink and to gamble. In this way he had made the acquaintance of Duval, an unscrupulous sharper, who had contrived to get away all his ready money, and persuading him to play longer in the hope of making up his losses had run him into debt one hundred and fifty dollars.

Dawkins gave him an acknowledgment of indebtedness to that amount. This of course placed him in Duval's power, since he knew of no means of raising such a sum. He therefore kept out of the Frenchman's way, avoiding the old haunts where he would have been likely to meet him. Dawkins supposed Duval ignorant of the whereabouts of his employer's counting-room. So he had been, but he made it his business to ascertain where it was. He had no idea of losing sight of so valuable a prize.

Dawkins would willingly have broken the appointment he had made with Duval, but he did not dare to do so. He knew that the man was well able to annoy him, and he would not on any account have had the affair disclosed to his father or Mr. Danforth.

As Trinity clock struck eight, he entered a low bar-room in the neighborhood of the docks.

A young man with pale, sandy hair stood behind the counter with his sleeves rolled up. He was supplying the wants of a sailor who already appeared to have taken more drink than was good for him.

"Good evening, Mr. Dawkins," said he, "you're a stranger."

"Is Duval in?" inquired Dawkins, coldly. His pride revolted at the place and company. He had never been here but once before, having met Duval elsewhere.

"He's up in his room. John show the young gentleman up to No. 9. Won't you have a glass of something this evening?"

"No," said Dawkins, abruptly.

The boy preceded him up a dark and dirty staircase.

"That's the room, sir," he said.

"Stop a minute," said Dawkins, "he may not be in."

He inwardly hoped he might not. But Duval answered his knock by coming to the door himself.

"Delighted to see you, mon ami. John, may leave the lamp. That's all, unless Mr. Dawkins wishes to order something."

"I want nothing," said Dawkins.

"They have some capital brandy."

"I am not in the mood for drinking tonight."

"As you please," said the Frenchman, disappointed; "be seated."

Dawkins sat down in a wooden rocking- chair, minus an arm.

"Well," said Duval, "how much money have you brought me?"

"None."

The Frenchman frowned and stroked his mustache, fiercely.

"What does all this mean? Are you going to put me off longer?"

"I would pay it if I could," said Dawkins, "but I haven't got the money."

"You could get it."

"How?"

"Ask your father."

"My father would rave if he knew that I had lost money in such a way."

"But you need not tell him."

"If I ask for money, he will be sure to ask what I want it for."

"Tell him you want clothes, or a watch, or a hundred things."

Dawkins shook his head; "it won't do," said he. "He wouldn't give me a hundred and fifty dollars."

"Then ask seventy-five, and I will wait a month for the rest."

"Look here, Duval, you have no rightful claim to this money. You've got enough out of me. Just tear up the paper."

Duval laughed scornfully, "Aha, Mr. Dawkins," he said, "that would be a very pretty arrangement FOR YOU. But I don't see how it is going to benefit me. No, no, I can't afford to throw away a hundred and fifty dollars so easily. If I was a rich man like your father it would make a difference."

"Then you won't remit the debt," said Dawkins, sullenly.

"You would think me a great ninny, if I did."

"Then you may collect it the best way you can."

"What do you mean by that?" demanded the Frenchman, his face darkening.

"I mean what I say," said Dawkins, desperately, "Gambling debts are not recognizable in law."

"Nothing is said about it's being a gambling debt. I have your note."

"Which is worth nothing, since I am a minor."

Duval's face became black with rage.

"Aha, my friend," said he showing his teeth, "this is a very nice game to cheat me out of my money. But it won't do, it won't do."

"Why won't it?"

"I shall say a word in your father's ear, mon ami, and in the ear of your worthy employer whom you were so anxious for me not to see, and perhaps that would be worse for you than to pay me my money."

Dawkins's brief exultation passed away. He saw that he was indeed in the power of an unscrupulous man, who was disposed to push his advantage to the utmost.

He subsided into a moody silence, which Duval watched with satisfaction.

"Well, my friend, what will you do about it?"

"I don't know what I can do."

"You will think of something. You will find it best," said the Frenchman, in a tone which veiled a threat.

"I will try," said Dawkins, gloomily.

"That is well. I thought you would listen to reason, mon ami. Now we will have a pleasant chat. Hold, I will order some brandy myself."

"Not for me," said Dawkins, rising from his chair, "I must be going."

"Will you not have one little game?" asked Duval, coaxingly.

"No, no, I have had enough of that. Goodnight."

"Then you won't stop. And when shall I have the pleasure of seeing you at my little apartment once more?"

"I don't know."

"If it is any trouble to you to come, I will call at your office," said Duval, significantly.

"Don't trouble yourself," said Dawkins, hastily; "I will come here a week from today."

"A week is a long time."

"Long or short, I must have it."

"Very well, mon ami. A week let it be. Good-night. Mind the stairs as you go down."

Dawkins breathed more freely as he passed out into the open air. He was beginning to realize that the way of the transgressor is hard.

XXX.

A TRAP IS LAID FOR PAUL.

Three months before, George Dawkins had made his first visit to a gambling house. At first, he had entered only from curiosity. He watched the play with an interest which gradually deepened, until he was easily persuaded to try his own luck. The stakes were small, but fortune favored him, and he came out some dollars richer than he entered. It would have been fortunate for him if he had failed. As it was, his good fortune encouraged him to another visit. This time he was less fortunate, but his gains about balanced his losses, so that he came out even. On the next occasion he left off with empty pockets. So it went on until at length he fell into the hands of Duval, who had no scruple in fleecing him to as great an extent as he could be induced to go.

George Dawkins's reflections were not of the most cheerful character as, leaving Duval, he slowly pursued his way homeward. He felt that he had fallen into the power of an unscrupulous villain, who would have no mercy upon him. He execrated his own folly, without which all the machination of Duval would have been without effect.

The question now, however, was, to raise the money. He knew of no one to whom he could apply except his father, nor did he have much hope from that quarter. Still, he would make the effort.

Reaching home he found his father seated in the library. He looked up from the evening paper as George entered.

"Only half-past nine," he said, with an air of sarcasm. "You spend your evenings out so systematically that your early return surprises me. How is it? Has the theater begun to lose its charm!"

There was no great sympathy between father and son, and if either felt affection for the other, it was never manifested. Mutual recrimination was the rule between them, and George would now have made an angry answer but that he had a favor to ask, and felt it politic to be conciliatory.

"If I had supposed you cared for my society, sir, I would have remained at home oftener."

"Umph!" was the only reply elicited from his father.

"However, there was a good reason for my not going to the theater to-night."

"Indeed!"

"I had no money."

"Your explanation is quite satisfactory," said his father, with a slight sneer. "I sympathize in your disappointment."

"There is no occasion, sir," said George, good humoredly, for him. "I had no great desire to go."

Dawkins took down a book from the library and tried to read, but without much success. His thoughts continually recurred to his pecuniary embarrassments, and the debt which he owed to Duval seemed to hang like a millstone around his neck. How should he approach his father on the subject? In his present humor he feared he would have little chance.

As his father laid down the newspaper Dawkins said, "Wouldn't you like a game of checkers, sir?"

This, as he well knew, was a favorite game with his father.

"I don't know but I should," said Mr. Dawkins, more graciously than was his wont.

The checker-board was brought, and the two commenced playing. Three games were played all of which his father won. This appeared to put him in a good humor, for as the two ceased playing, he drew a ten-dollar-bill from his pocket-book, and handed to his son, with the remark, "There, George, I don't want you to be penniless. You are a little extravagant, though, I think. Your pay from Mr. Danforth ought to keep you in spending money."

"Yes, sir, I have been rather extravagant, but I am going to reform."

"I am very glad to hear it."

"I wish, sir," said George a moment afterwards," that you would allow me to buy my own clothes."

"I've no sort of an objection, I am sure. You select them now, don't you?"

"Yes, sir, but I mean to suggest that you should make me an allowance for that purpose, —about as much as it costs now,—and give me the money to spend where I please."

Mr. Dawkins looked sharply at his son.

"The result would probably be," he said, "that the money would be expended in other ways, and I should have to pay for the clothes twice over."

Dawkins would have indignantly disclaimed this, if he had not felt that he was not altogether sincere in the request he had made.

"No," continued his father, "I don't like the arrangement you propose. When you need clothing you can go to my tailor and order it, of course not exceeding reasonable limits."

"But," said Dawkins, desperately, "I don't like Bradshaw's style of making clothes. I would prefer trying some other tailor."

"What fault have you to find with Bradshaw? Is he not one of the most fashionable tailors in the city?"

"Yes, sir, I suppose so, but——"

"Come, sir, you are growing altogether too particular. All your garments set well, so far as I can judge."

"Yes, sir, but one likes a change sometimes," persisted George, a little embarrassed for further objections.

"Well," said Mr. Dawkins, after a pause, "If you are so strongly bent upon a new tailor, select one, and order what you need. You can tell him to send in his bill to me."

"Thank you sir," said his son, by no means pleased at the manner in which his request had been granted. He saw that it would in no manner promote the plan which he had in view, since it would give him no command of the ready money. It is hardly necessary to say that his alleged dissatisfaction with his father's tailor had all been trumped up for the occasion, and would never have been thought of but for the present emergency.

"What shall I do!" thought Dawkins, in perplexity, as he slowly undressed himself and retired to bed.

The only true course, undoubtedly, was to confess all to his father, to incur the storm of reproaches which would have followed as the just penalty of his transgression, and then the haunting fear of discovery would have been once and forever removed. But Dawkins was not brave enough for this. He thought only of escaping from his present difficulty without his father's knowledge.

He rose the next morning with the burden of care still weighing upon him. In the evening the thought occurred to him that he might retrieve his losses where he had incurred them, and again he bent his steps to the gambling house. He risked five dollars, being one-half of what he had. This was lost. Desperately he hazarded the remaining five dollars, and lost again.

With a muttered oath he sprang to his feet, and left the brilliant room, more gloomy and discouraged than ever. He was as badly off as before, and penniless beside. He would have finished the evening at the theater, but his recent loss prevented that. He lounged about the streets till it was time to go to bed, and then went home in a very unsatisfactory state of mind.

A day or two after, he met on Broadway the man whom of all others he would gladly have avoided.

"Aha, my friend, I am glad to meet you," said Duval, for it was he.

Dawkins muttered something unintelligible, and would have hurried on, but Duval detained him.

"Why are you in such a hurry, my friend?" he said.

"Business," returned Dawkins, shortly.

"That reminds me of the little business affair between us, mon ami. Have you got any money for me?"

"Not yet."

"Not yet! It is three days since we saw each other. Could you not do something in three days?"

"I told you I required a week," said Dawkins, roughly, "Let go my arm. I tell you I am in haste."

"Very well, mon ami," said Duval, slowly relinquishing his hold, "take care that you do not forget. There are four days more to the week."

Dawkins hurried on feeling very uncomfortable. He was quite aware that four days hence he would be as unprepared to encounter the Frenchman as now. Still, something might happen.

Something, unfortunately, did happen.

The next day Mr. Danforth was counting a roll of bills which had been just paid in, when he was unexpectedly called out of the counting-room. He unguardedly left the bills upon his own desk. Dawkins saw them lying there. The thought flashed upon him, "There lies what will relieve me from all my embarrassment."

Allowing himself scarcely a minute to think, he took from the roll four fifty dollar notes, thrust one into the pocket of Paul's overcoat, which hung up in the office, drew off his right boot and slipped the other three into the bottom of it, and put it on again. He then nervously resumed his place at his desk. A moment afterwards, Paul, who had been to the post-office, entered with letters which he carried into the inner office and deposited on Mr. Danforth's desk. He observed the roll of bills, and thought his employer careless in leaving so much money exposed, but said nothing on the subject to Dawkins, between whom and himself there was little communication.

XXXI.

CONVICTED OF THEFT.

Half an hour later Mr. Danforth returned.

"Has any one been here?" he asked as he passed through the outer office.

"No, sir," said Dawkins, with outward composure though his heart was beating rapidly.

While apparently intent upon his writing he listened attentively to what might be going on in the next room. One,—two,—three minutes passed. Mr. Danforth again showed himself.

"Did you say that no one has been here?" he demanded, abruptly.

"No, sir."

"Have either of you been into my office since I have been out?"

"I have not, sir," said Dawkins.

"I went in to carry your letters," said Paul.

"Did you see a roll of bills lying on my desk?"

"Yes, sir," said Paul, a little surprised at the question.

"I have just counted it over, and find but six hundred dollars instead of eight hundred. Can you account for the discrepancy?"

Mr. Danforth looked keenly at the two boys. Dawkins, who had schooled himself to the ordeal, maintained his outward calmness. Paul, beginning to perceive that his honesty was called in question, flushed.

"No, sir," said the boys simultaneously.

"It can hardly be possible, that Mr. Thompson, who is a very careful man, should have made such a mistake in paying me," resumed Mr. Danforth.

"As we have been the only persons here," said Dawkins, "the only way to vindicate ourselves from suspicion is, to submit to a search."

"Yes, sir," said Paul promptly.

Both boys turned their pockets inside out, but the missing money was not found.

"There is my overcoat, sir," said Dawkins, "will you be kind enough to search it for yourself?"

Next, of course, Paul's overcoat was searched.

What was our hero's dismay when from one of the pockets Mr. Danforth produced a fifty dollar bill.

"Is it possible?" he exclaimed in as much grief as surprise, "Unhappy boy, how came you by this money in your pocket?"

"I don't know, sir," returned Paul, his cheek alternately flushing and growing pale.

"I wish I could believe you," said Mr. Danforth; "where have you put the other bills? Produce them, and I may overlook this first offense."

"Indeed, sir," said Paul, in great distress, "I have not the slightest knowledge of how this bill came into my pocket. I hope you will believe me, sir."

"How can I? The money evidently did not go into your pocket without hands."

A sudden thought came to Paul. "Dawkins," said he, "did you put that money into my pocket?"

"What do you mean, sir?" returned Dawkins, haughtily. "Is it your intention to insult me?"

Dawkins could not prevent his face from flushing as he spoke, but this might easily be referred to a natural resentment of the imputation cast upon him.

"Paul," said his employer, coldly, "you will not help your own cause by seeking to involve another. After what has happened you can hardly expect me to retain you in my employment. I will not make public your disgrace, nor will I inquire farther for the remainder of the money for which you have been willing to barter your integrity. I will pay your wages up to the end of this week, and——"

"Mr. Danforth," said Paul, manfully, though the tears almost choked his utterance, "I am sorry that you have no better opinion of me. I do not want the balance of my wages. If I have taken so large a sum which did not belong to me, I have no claim to them. Good-morning, sir. Sometime I hope you will think better of me."

Paul put on his coat, and taking his cap from the nail on which it hung, bowed respectfully to his employer and left the office.

Mr. Danforth looked after him, and seemed perplexed. Could Paul be guilty after all?

"I never could have suspected him if I had not this evidence in my hand," said Mr. Danforth, to himself, fixing his eyes upon the bill which he had drawn from Paul's overcoat.

"Dawkins, did you observe whether Paul remained long in the office?" he asked,

"Longer than sufficient to lay the letters on the desk?"

"Yes, sir, I think he did."

"Did you notice whether he went to his overcoat after coming out?"

"Yes, sir, he did," said Dawkins, anxious to fix in Mr. Danforth's mind the impression of Paul's guilt.

"Then I am afraid it is true," said his employer sadly. "And yet, what a fine, manly boy he is too. But it is a terrible fault."

Mr. Danforth was essentially a kind-hearted man, and he cared much more for Paul's dereliction from honesty than for the loss of the money. Going home early to dinner, he communicated to his wife the unpleasant discovery which he had made respecting Paul.

Now, from the first, Paul had been a great favorite with Mrs. Danforth, and she scouted at the idea of his dishonesty.

"Depend upon it, Mr. Danforth," she said decisively, "you have done the boy an injustice. I have some skill in reading faces, and I tell you that a boy with Paul Prescott's open, frank expression is incapable of such a crime."

"So I should have said, my dear, but we men learn to be less trustful than you ladies, who stay at home and take rose-colored views of life. Unfortunately, we see too much of the dark side of human nature."

"So that you conclude all to be dark."

"Not so bad as that."

"Tell me all the circumstances, and perhaps a woman's wit may help you."

Mr. Danforth communicated all the details, with which the reader is already familiar.

"What sort of a boy is this Dawkins?" she asked, "Do you like him?"

"Not particularly. He does his duties passably well. I took him into my counting-room to oblige his father."

"Perhaps he is the thief."

"To tell the truth I would sooner have suspected him."

"Has he cleared himself from suspicion?"

"He was the first to suggest a search."

"Precisely the thing he would have done, if he had placed the bill in Paul's pocket. Of course he would know that the search must result favorably for him."

"There is something in that."

"Besides, what could have been more foolish, if Paul wished to hide the money, than to multiply his chances of detection by hiding it in two different places, especially where one was so obvious as to afford no concealment at all."

"Admitting this to be true, how am I to arrive at the proof of Paul's innocence?"

"My own opinion is, that George Dawkins has the greater part of the money stolen. Probably he has taken it for some particular purpose. What it is, you may learn, perhaps, by watching him."

"I will be guided by your suggestion. Nothing would afford me greater pleasure than to find that I have been mistaken in assuming Paul's guilt, though on evidence that seemed convincing."

This conversation took place at the dinner- table. Mr. Danforth understood that no time was to be lost if he expected to gain any information from the movements of his clerk.

George Dawkins had ventured upon a bold act, but he had been apparently favored by fortune, and had succeeded. That he should have committed this crime without compunction could hardly be expected. His uneasiness, however, sprang chiefly from the fear that in some way he might yet be detected. He resolved to get rid of the money which he had obtained dishonestly, and obtain back from Duval the acknowledgment of indebtedness which he had given him.

You will perhaps ask whether the wrong which he had done Paul affected him with uneasiness. On the contrary, it gratified the dislike which from the first he had cherished towards our hero.

"I am well rid of him, at all events," he muttered to himself, "that is worth risking some thing for."

When office hours were over Dawkins gladly threw down his pen, and left the counting-room.

He bent his steps rapidly towards the locality where he had before met Duval. He had decided to wait some time before meeting that worthy. He had to wait till another day, when as he was emerging from the tavern he encountered the Frenchman on the threshold.

"Aha, my good friend," said Duval, offering his hand, which Dawkins did not appear to see, "I am very glad to see you. Will you come in?"

"No, I have not time," said Dawkins, shortly.

"Have you brought me my money?"

"Yes."

"Aha, that is well. I was just about what you call cleaned out."

"Have you my note with you?"

Duval fumbled in his pocket-book, and finally produced the desired document.

"Give it to me."

"I must have the money first," said the Frenchman, shrewdly.

"Take it," said Dawkins contemptuously. "Do you judge me by yourself?"

He tore the note which he received into small pieces, and left Duval without another word.

Sheltered by the darkness, Mr. Danforth, who had tracked the steps of Dawkins, had been an unseen witness of this whole transaction.

XXXII.

RIGHT TRIUMPHANT.

George Dawkins resumed his duties the next morning as usual. Notwithstanding the crime he had committed to screen himself from the consequences of a lighter fault, he felt immeasurably relieved at the thought that he had shaken himself free from the clutches of Duval. His satisfaction was heightened by the disgrace and summary dismissal of Paul, whom he had never liked. He decided to ask the place for a cousin of his own, whose society would be more agreeable to him than that of his late associate.

"Good-morning, sir," he said, as Mr. Danforth entered.

"Good-morning," returned his employer, coldly.

"Have you selected any one in Prescott's place, yet, sir?"

"Why do you ask?"

"Because I have a cousin, Malcolm Harcourt, who would be glad to take it."

"Indeed!" said Mr. Danforth, whose manner somewhat puzzled Dawkins.

"I should enjoy having him with me," continued Dawkins.

"Did you like Prescott?"

"No, sir," said Dawkins, promptly, "I didn't want to say so before, but now, since he's turned out so badly, I don't mind saying that I never thought much of him."

"On the contrary," said Mr. Danforth, "I liked him from the first. Perhaps we are wrong in thinking that he took the money."

"I should think there could be no doubt of it," said Dawkins, not liking the sympathy and returning good feeling for Paul which his employer manifested.

"I don't agree with you," said Mr. Danforth, coldly. "I have decided to reinstate Paul in his former place."

"Then, if any more money is missing, you will know where it has gone," said Dawkins, hastily.

"I shall."

"Then there is no chance for my cousin?"

"I am expecting to have a vacancy."

Dawkins looked up in surprise.

"I shall require some one to fill YOUR place," said Mr. Danforth, significantly.

"Sir!" exclaimed Dawkins, in astonishment and dismay.

His employer bent a searching glance upon him as he asked, sternly, "where did you obtain the money which you paid away last evening?"

"I—don't—understand—you, sir," gasped Dawkins, who understood only too well.

"You met a man at the door of a low tavern in—Street, last evening, to whom you paid one hundred and fifty dollars, precisely the sum which I lost yesterday."

"Who has been slandering me, sir?" asked Dawkins, very pale.

"An eye-witness of the meeting, who heard the conversation between you. If you want more satisfactory proof, here it is."

Mr. Danforth took from his pocket-book the torn fragments of the note which Dawkins had given to Duval.

"Here is an obligation to pay a certain Duval the sum of one hundred and fifty dollars. It bears your signature. How you could have incurred such a debt to him you best know."

Dawkins maintained a sullen silence.

"I suppose you wish me to leave your employment," he said at length.

"You are right. Hold," he added, as Dawkins was about leaving the room, "a word more. It is only just that you should make a restitution of the sum which you have taken. If you belonged to a poor family and there were extenuating circumstances, I might forego my claim. But your father is abundantly able to make good the loss, and I shall require you to lay the matter before him without loss of time. In consideration of your youth, I shall not bring the matter before the public tribunals, as I have a right to do."

Dawkins turned pale at this allusion, and muttering some words to the effect that he would do what he could, left the counting-room.

This threat proved not to be without its effect. The next day he came to Mr. Danforth and brought the sum for which he had become responsible. He had represented to his father that he had had his pocket picked of this sum belonging to Mr. Danforth, and in that manner obtained an equal amount to replace it. It was some time before Mr. Dawkins learned the truth. Then came a storm of reproaches in which all the bitterness of his father's nature was fully exhibited. There had never been much love between father and son. Henceforth there was open hatred.

We must return to Paul, whom we left in much trouble.

It was a sad walk which he took homeward on the morning of his dismissal.

"What brings you home so early?" asked Mrs. Cameron, looking up from her baking, as Paul entered.

Paul tried to explain, but tears came to his eyes, and sobs choked his utterance.

"Are you sick, Paul?" exclaimed Mrs. Cameron, in alarm.

"No, Aunt Hester."

"Then what is the matter?" she asked anxiously.

"I have lost my place."

"Poor boy! I am very sorry to hear it. But it might have been worse."

"No, not very well, Aunt Hester, for Mr. Danforth thinks I have taken some of his money."

"He is very unjust!" exclaimed Aunt Hester, indignantly, "he ought to have known better than to think you would steal."

"Why, no," said Paul, candidly, "I must confess the evidence was against me, and he doesn't know me as well as you do, Aunt Hester."

"Tell me all about it, Paul."

Aunt Hester sat down and listened attentively to our hero's story.

"How do you account for the money being found in your pocket?" she asked at length.

"I think it must have been put there by some one else."

"Have you any suspicions?"

"Yes," said Paul, a little reluctantly, "but I don't know whether I ought to have. I may be wronging an innocent person."

"At any rate it won't do any harm to tell me."

"You've heard me speak of George Dawkins?"

"Yes."

"I can't help thinking that he put the fifty dollars into my pocket, and took the rest himself."

"How very wicked he must be!" exclaimed Mrs. Cameron, indignantly.

"Don't judge him too hastily; Aunt Hester, he may not be guilty, and I know from my own experience how hard it is to be accused when you are innocent."

Soon after the sexton came in, and Paul of course, told his story over again.

"Never mind, Paul," said Uncle Hugh, cheerily. "You know your own innocence; that is the main thing. It's a great thing to have a clear conscience."

"But I liked Mr. Danforth and I think he liked me. It's hard to feel that he and Mrs. Danforth will both think me guilty, especially after the kindness which I have experienced from them."

"We all have our crosses, my boy,—some light and others heavy. Yours, I admit is a heavy one for a boy to bear. But when men are unjust there is One above who will deal justly with us. You have not forgotten him."

"No, Uncle Hugh," said Paul, reverently.

"Trust in him, Paul, and all will come out right at last. He can prove your innocence, and you may be sure he will, in his own good time. Only be patient, Paul."

"I will try to be, Uncle Hugh."

The simple, hearty trust in God, which the sexton manifested, was not lost upon Paul. Sustained by his own consciousness of innocence, and the confidence reposed in him by those who knew him best, his mind soon regained its cheerful tone. He felt an inward conviction that God would vindicate his innocence.

His vindication came sooner than he anticipated.

The next day as the sexton's family were seated at their plain dinner, a knock was heard upon the outer door.

"Sit still, Hester," said Mr. Cameron. "I will go to the door."

Opening the door he recognized Mr. Danforth, who attended the same church.

"Mr. Cameron, I believe," said Mr. Danforth, pleasantly.

"Yes, sir."

"May I come in? I am here on a little business."

"Certainly, Mr. Danforth. Excuse my not inviting you before; but in my surprise at seeing you, I forgot my politeness."

The sexton led the way into the plain sitting-room.

"I believe Paul Prescott is an inmate of your family."

"Yes, sir. I am sorry——"

"I know what you would say, sir; but it is needless. May I see Paul a moment?"

Paul was surprised at the summons, and still more surprised at finding who it was that wished to see him.

He entered the room slowly, uncertain how to accost Mr. Danforth. His employer solved the doubt in his mind by advancing cordially, and taking his hand.

"Paul," he said pleasantly, "I have come here to ask your forgiveness for an injustice, and to beg you to resume your place in my counting-room."

"Have you found out who took the money, sir?" asked Paul, eagerly.

"Yes."

"Who was it, sir?"

"It was Dawkins."

Mr. Danforth explained how he had become acquainted with the real thief. In conclusion, he said, "I shall expect you back to-morrow morning, Paul."

"Thank you, sir."

"Dawkins of course leaves my employ. You will take his place, and receive his salary, seven dollars a week instead of five. Have you any friend whom you would like to have in your own place?"

Paul reflected a moment and finally named a schoolmate of his, the son of poor parents, whom he knew to be anxiously seeking a situation, but without influential friends to help him.

"I will take him on your recommendation," said Mr. Danforth, promptly. "Can you see him this afternoon?"

"Yes, sir," said Paul.

The next day Paul resumed his place in Mr. Danforth's counting-room.

XXXIII.

PAUL REDEEMS HIS PLEDGE.

Two years passed, unmarked by any incident of importance. Paul continued in Mr. Danforth's employment, giving, if possible, increased satisfaction. He was not only faithful, but exhibited a rare aptitude for business, which made his services of great value to his employer. From time to time Mr. Danforth increased his salary, so that, though only nineteen, he was now receiving twelve dollars per week, with the prospect of a speedy increase. But with his increasing salary, he did not increase his expenses. He continued as economical as ever. He had not forgotten his father's dying injunction. He remained true to the charge which he had taken upon himself, that of redeeming his father's memory from reproach. This, at times subjected him to the imputation of meanness, but for this he cared little. He would not swerve from the line of duty which he had marked out.

One evening as he was walking down Broadway with an acquaintance, Edward Hastings, who was employed in a counting-room near him, they paused before a transparency in front of a hall brilliantly lighted.

"The Hutchinsons are going to sing to-night, Paul," said Hastings. "Did you ever hear them?"

"No; but I have often wished to."

"Then suppose we go in." "No, I believe not."

"Why not. Paul? It seems to me you never go anywhere. You ought to amuse yourself now and then."

"Some other time I will,—not now."

"You are not required to be at home in the evening, are you?"

"No."

"Then why not come in now? It's only twenty-five cents."

"To tell the truth, Ned, I am saving up my money for a particular purpose; and until that is accomplished, I avoid all unnecessary expense."

"Going to invest in a house in Fifth Avenue? When you do, I'll call. However, never mind the expense. I'll pay you in."

"I'm much obliged to you, Ned, but I can't. accept."

"Why not?"

"Because at present I can't afford to return the favor."

"Never mind that."

"But I do mind it. By-and-by I shall feel more free. Good-night, if you are going in."

"Good-night, Paul."

"He's a strange fellow," mused Hastings.

"It's impossible to think him mean, and yet, it looks a great deal like it. He spends nothing for dress or amusements. I do believe that I've had three coats since he's been wearing that old brown one. Yet, he always looks neat. I wonder what he's saving up his money for."

Meanwhile Paul went home.

The sexton and his wife looked the same as ever. Paul sometimes fancied that Uncle Hugh stooped a little more than he used to do; but his life moved on so placidly and evenly, that he grew old but slowly. Aunt Hester was the same good, kind, benevolent friend that she had always been. No mother could have been more devoted to Paul. He felt that he had much to be grateful for, in his chance meeting with this worthy couple.

It was the first of January,—a clear, cold day. A pleasant fire burned in the little stove. Mr. Cameron sat at one side, reading the evening paper; Mrs. Cameron at the other, knitting a stocking for Paul. A large, comfortable- looking cat was dozing tranquilly on the hearth-rug. Paul, who had been seated at the table, rose and lighted a candle.

"Where are you going, Paul?" asked Aunt Hester.

"Up-stairs for a moment."

Paul speedily returned, bearing in his hand a small blue bank-book, with his name on the cover.

He took out his pencil and figured a few minutes.

"Uncle Hugh," said he, looking up, "when I get a hundred dollars more, I shall have enough to pay father's debt."

"Principal and interest?"

"Yes, principal and interest; reckoning the interest for a year to come."

"I did not suppose you had so much money, Paul. You must have been very economical."

"Yes, Uncle Hugh more so than I have wanted to be, oftentimes; but whenever I have been tempted to spend a cent unnecessarily, I have always called to mind my promise made to father on his deathbed, and I have denied myself."

"You have done well, Paul. There are few who would have had the resolution to do as you have."

"Oh yes, Uncle Hugh," said Paul, modestly, "I think there are a great many. I begin to feel repaid already. In a few months I shall be able to pay up the whole debt."

At this moment a knock was heard at the door. Mr. Cameron answered the summons.

"Does Mr. Paul Prescott live here?" inquired a boy.

"Yes. Do you want to see him?"

"Here is a letter for him. There is no answer."

The messenger departed, leaving the letter in Mr. Cameron's hand.

Somewhat surprised, he returned to the sitting-room and handed it to Paul.

Paul opened it hastily, and discovered inclosed, a bank-note for one hundred dollars. It was accompanied with a note from his employer, stating that it was intended as a New Year's gift, but in the hurry of business, he had forgotten to give it to him during the day.

Paul's face lighted up with joy.

"Oh, Uncle Hugh!" he exclaimed, almost breathless with delight. "Don't you see that this will enable me to pay my debt at once?"

"So it will, Paul. I wish you joy."

"And my father's memory will be vindicated," said Paul, in a tone of deep satisfaction. "If he could only have lived to see this day!"

A fortnight later, Paul obtained permission from his employer to be absent from the office for a week. It was his purpose to visit Cedarville and repay 'Squire Conant the debt due him: and then, to go across the country to Wrenville, thirty miles distant, to see Aunt Lucy Lee. First, however, he ordered a new suit of a tailor, feeling a desire to appear to the best advantage on his return to the scene of his former humiliation. I must not omit to say that Paul was now a fine-looking young fellow of nineteen, with a frank, manly face, that won favor wherever he went.

In due course of time, he arrived at Cedarville, and found his way without difficulty to the house of 'Squire Conant.

It was a large house, rather imposing in its exterior, being quite the finest residence in the village.

Paul went up the walk, and rang the bell.

"Can I see 'Squire Conant?" he asked of the servant who answered the bell.

"You'll find him in that room," said the girl, pointing to a door on the left hand of the hall.

"As he doesn't know me, perhaps you had better go before."

The door was opened, and Paul found himself in the presence of his father's creditor. 'Squire Conant was looking pale and thin. He was just recovering from a severe sickness.

"I presume you don't recognize me, sir," said Paul.

"Did I ever see you before?"

"Yes, sir; my name is Paul Prescott."

"Not the son of John Prescott?"

"The same, sir. I believe my father died in your debt."

"Yes. I lent him five hundred dollars, which he never repaid."

"He tried to do so, sir. He had saved up a hundred and fifty dollars towards it, but sickness came upon him, and he was obliged to use it."

'Squire Conant's temper had been subdued by the long and dangerous illness through which he had passed. It had made him set a smaller value on his earthly possessions, from which he might be separated at any moment. When he answered Paul, it was in a manner which our hero did not expect.

"Never mind. I can afford to lose it. I have no doubt he did what he could."

"But I have come to pay it, sir," said Paul.

"You!" exclaimed 'Squire Conant, in the greatest astonishment.

"Yes, sir."

"Where did you get the money?"

"I earned it, sir."

"But you are very young. How could you have earned so much?"

Paul frankly told the story of his struggles; how for years he had practised a pinch-
ing economy, in order to redeem his father's memory from reproach.

'Squire Conant listened attentively.

"You are a good boy," he said, at length.

"Shall you have anything left after paying this money?"

"No, sir; but I shall soon earn more."

"Still, you ought to have something to begin the world with. You shall pay me
half the money, and I will cancel the note."

"But, sir,——"

"Not a word. I am satisfied, and that is enough. If I hadn't lent your father the
money, I might have invested it with the rest, and lost all."

'Squire Conant produced the note from a little trunk of papers, and handed it to
Paul, who paid him the amount which he had stipulated, expressing at the same
time his gratitude for his unexpected generosity.

"Never mind about thanks, my boy," said 'Squire Conant: "I am afraid I have
loved money too well heretofore. I hope I am not too old to turn over a new leaf."

XXXIV.

HOW PAUL GOES BACK TO WRENVILLE.

While 'Squire Conant was speaking, Paul formed a sudden resolution. He remembered that Aunt Lucy Lee was a sister of 'Squire Conant. Perhaps, in his present frame of mind, it might be possible to induce him to do something for her.

"I believe I am acquainted with a sister of yours, 'Squire Conant," he commenced.

"Ha!" exclaimed the 'Squire.

"Mrs. Lucy Lee."

"Yes," was the slow reply; "she is my sister. Where did you meet her?"

"At the Wrenville Poorhouse."

"How long ago?"

"About six years since."

"Is she there, still?"

"Yes, sir. Since I have been in New York, I have heard from her frequently. I am going from here to visit her. Have you any message, sir? I am sure she would be glad to hear from you."

"She shall hear from me," said the 'Squire in a low voice. "Sit down, and I will write her a letter which, I hope, will not prove unwelcome."

Five minutes afterwards he handed Paul an open letter.

"You may read it," he said, abruptly.

"You have been a better friend to my sister than I. You shall witness my late reparation."

The letter was as follows:—— MY DEAR SISTER:— CEDARVILLE, JAN 13, 18—.

I hope you will forgive me for my long neglect. It is not fitting that while I am possessed of abundant means you should longer remain the tenant of an almshouse. I send you by the bearer of this note, Paul Prescott, who, I understand, is a friend of yours, the sum of three hundred dollars. The same sum will be sent you annually. I hope it will be sufficient to maintain you comfortably. I shall endeavor to call upon you soon, and meanwhile remain, Your affectionate brother

EZEKIEL CONANT.

Paul read this letter with grateful joy. It seemed almost to good to be true. Aunt Lucy would be released from the petty tyranny of Mrs. Mudge's household, and perhaps—he felt almost sure Aunt Hester would be willing to receive her as a boarder, thus insuring her a peaceful and happy home in her declining years.

"Oh, sir," said he, seizing 'Squire Conant's hand, "you cannot tell how happy you have made me."

"It is what I ought to have done before. Here is the money referred to in the letter,— three hundred dollars,—mind you don't lose it."

"I will take every care, sir."

"You may tell my sister that I shall be happy to have her write me."

"I will, sir."

Paul left 'Squire Conant's house, feeling that he had great cause for joy. The 'Squire's refusal to receive more than half the debt, left him master of over three hundred dollars. But I am not sure whether he did not rejoice even more over the good fortune which had come to Aunt Lucy Lee, whose kindness to him, in his unfriended boyhood, he would ever hold in grateful remembrance. He enjoyed in anticipation the joy which he knew Aunt Lucy would feel when the change in her fortunes was communicated to her. He knew also how great would be the chagrin of Mr. and Mrs. Mudge, when they found that the meek old lady whom they hated was about to be rescued from their clutches. On the whole, Paul felt that this was the happiest day of his life. It was a satisfaction to feel that the good fortune of his early friend was all due to his own intercession.

He was able to take the cars to a point four miles distant from Wrenville. On getting out on the platform he inquired whether there was a livery stable near by. He was directed to one but a few rods distant. Entering he asked, "Can you let me have a horse and chaise to go to Wrenville?"

"Yes, sir," said the groom.

"Let me have the best horse in the stable," said Paul, "and charge me accordingly."

"Yes, sir," said the groom, respectfully, judging from Paul's dress and tone that he was a young gentleman of fortune.

A spirited animal was brought out, and Paul was soon seated in the chaise driving along the Wrenville road. Paul's city friends would hardly have recognized their economical acquaintance in the well-dressed young man who now sat behind a fast horse, putting him through his best paces. It might have been a weakness in Paul, but he remembered the manner in which he left Wrenville, an unfriended boy, compelled to fly from persecution under the cover of darkness, and he felt a certain pride in showing the Mudges that his circumstances were now entirely changed. It was over this very road that he had walked with his little bundle, in the early morning, six years before. It seemed to him almost like a dream.

At length he reached Wrenville. Though he had not been there for six years, he recognized the places that had once been familiar to him. But everything seemed to have dwindled. Accustomed to large city warehouses, the houses in the village seemed very diminutive. Even 'Squire Benjamin Newcome's house, which he had once regarded as a stately mansion, now looked like a very ordinary dwelling.

As he rode up the main street of the village, many eyes were fixed upon him and his carriage, but no one thought of recognizing, in the well-dressed youth, the boy who had run away from the Wrenville Poorhouse.

XXXV.

CONCLUSION.

At the very moment that Paul was driving through the village street, Mr. Nicholas Mudge entered the Poorhouse in high spirits. Certainly ill-fortune must have befallen some one to make the good man so exhilarant.

To explain, Mr. Mudge had just been to the village store to purchase some groceries. One of his parcels was tied up in a stray leaf of a recent New York Daily, in which he discovered an item which he felt sure would make Aunt Lucy unhappy. He communicated it to Mrs. Mudge, who highly approved his design. She called the old lady from the common room.

"Here, Aunt Lucy," she said, "is something that will interest you."

Aunt Lucy came in, wondering a little at such an unusual mark of attention.

Mrs. Mudge immediately commenced reading with malicious emphasis a paragraph concerning a certain Paul Prescott, who had been arrested for thieving, and sentenced to the House of Reformation for a term of months.

"There," said Mrs. Mudge, triumphantly, "what do you say to your favorite now? Turned out well, hasn't he? Didn't I always say so? I always knew that boy was bad at heart, and that he'd come to a bad end."

"I don't believe it's the same boy," declared Aunt Lucy, who was nevertheless unpleasantly affected by the paragraph. She thought it possible that Paul might have yielded to a powerful temptation.

"Perhaps you think I've been making it up. If you don't believe it look at the paper for yourself," thrusting it into Aunt Lucy's hands.

"Yes," said the old lady. "I see that the name is the same; but, for all that, there is a mistake somewhere. I do not believe it is the same boy."

"You don't? Just as if there would be more than one boy of that name. There may be other Prescotts, but there isn't but one Paul Prescott, take my word for it."

"If it is he," said Aunt Lucy, indignantly, "is it Christianlike to rejoice over the poor boy's misfortune?"

"Misfortune!" retorted Mrs. Mudge with a sneer; "you call it a misfortune to steal, then! I call it a crime."

"It's often misfortune that drives people to it, though," continued the old lady, looking keenly at Mrs. Mudge. "I have known cases where they didn't have that excuse."

Mrs. Mudge colored.

"Go back to your room," said she, sharply; "and don't stay here accusing me and Mr. Mudge of unchristian conduct. You're the most troublesome pauper we have on our hands; and I do wish the town would provide for you somewhere else."

"So do I," sighed the old lady to herself, though she did not think fit to give audible voice to her thoughts.

It was at this moment that Paul halted his chaise at the gate, and lightly jumping out, fastened his horse to a tree, and walked up to the front door.

"Who can it be?" thought Mrs. Mudge, hastily adjusting her cap, and taking off her apron.

"I don't know, I'm sure," said Mr. Mudge, unsuspiciously.

"I declare! I look like a fright."

"No worse than usual," said her husband, gallantly.

By this time Paul had knocked.

Good-morning, sir," said Mrs. Mudge, deferentially, her respect excited by Paul's dress and handsome chaise.

"Is Mrs. Lee in?" inquired Paul, not caring to declare himself, yet, to his old enemy.

"Yes," said Mrs. Mudge, obsequiously, though not overpleased to find that this was Aunt Lucy's visitor; "would you like to see her?"

"If you please."

"What can he want of the old lady?" thought Mrs. Mudge, as she went to summon her.

"A visitor for me?" asked Aunt Lucy, looking at Mrs. Mudge somewhat suspiciously.

"Yes; and as he's come in a carriage, you'd better slick up a little; put on a clean cap or something."

Aunt Lucy was soon ready.

She looked wonderingly at Paul, not recognizing him.

"You are not very good at remembering your old friends," said Paul, with a smile.

"What!" exclaimed Aunt Lucy, her face lighting up with joy; "are you little Paul?"

"Not very little, now," said our hero, laughing; "but I'm the same Paul you used to know."

Mrs. Mudge, who through the half open door had heard this revelation, was overwhelmed with astonishment and confusion. She hurried to her husband.

"Wonders will never cease!" she exclaimed, holding up both hands. "If that doesn't turn out to be Paul Prescott. Of course he's up in the world, or he wouldn't dress so well, and ride in such a handsome carriage."

"You don't say so!" returned Mr. Mudge, who looked as if he had heard of a heavy misfortune.

"Yes, I do; I heard him say so with his own lips. It's a pity you showed that paragraph to Aunt Lucy, this morning."

"That you showed, you mean," retorted her husband.

"No, I don't. You know it was you that did it."

"Hush; they'll hear."

Meanwhile the two friends were conversing together happily.

"I'm so glad you're doing so well, Paul," said Aunt Lucy. "It was a lucky day when you left the Poorhouse behind you."

"Yes, Aunt Lucy, and to-day is a lucky day for you. There's room for two in that chaise, and I'm going to take you away with me."

"I should enjoy a ride, Paul. It's a long time since I have taken one."

"You don't understand me. You're going away not to return."

The old lady smiled sadly.

"No, no, Paul. I can't consent to become a burden upon your generosity. You can't afford it, and it will not be right."

"O," said Paul, smiling, "you give me credit for too much. I mean that you shall pay your board."

"But you know I have no money."

"No, I don't. I don't consider that a lady is penniless, who has an income of three hundred dollars a year."

"I don't understand you, Paul."

"Then, perhaps you will understand this," said our hero, enjoying the old lady's astonishment.

He drew from his pocket a roll of bills, and passed them to Aunt Lucy.

The old lady looked so bewildered, that he lost no time in explaining the matter to her. Then, indeed, Aunt Lucy was happy; not only because she had become suddenly independent, but, because after years of coldness and estrangement, her brother had at last become reconciled to her.

"Now, Aunt Lucy," resumed Paul, "I'll tell you what my plans are. You shall get into the chaise with me, and go at once to New York. I think Aunt Hester will be willing to receive you as a boarder; if not, I will find you a pleasant place near by. Will that suit you?"

"It will make me very happy; but I cannot realize it. It seems like a dream."

At this moment Mrs. Mudge entered the room, and, after a moment's scrutiny, pretended to recognize Paul. Her husband followed close behind her.

"Can I believe my eyes?" she exclaimed. "Is this indeed Paul Prescott? I am very glad to see you back."

"Only a visit, Mrs. Mudge," said Paul, smiling.

"You'll stop to dinner, I hope?"

Paul thought of the soup and dry bread which he used to find so uninviting, and said that he should not have time to do so.

"We've thought of you often," said Mr. Mudge, writhing his harsh features into a smile. "There's scarcely a day that we haven't spoken of you."

"I ought to feel grateful for your remembrance," said Paul, his eyes twinkling with mirth. "But I don't think, Mr. Mudge, you always thought so much of me."

Mr. Mudge coughed in some embarrassment, and not thinking of anything in particular to say, said nothing.

"I am going to take from you another of your boarders," said Paul. "Can you spare Aunt Lucy?"

"For how long?" asked Mrs. Mudge.

"For all the time. She has just come into possession of a little property,—several hundred dollars a year,—and I have persuaded her to go to New York to board."

"Is this true?" exclaimed Mrs. Mudge in astonishment.

"Yes," said the old lady, "God has been bountiful to me when I least expected it."

"Can I be of any service in assisting you to pack up, Mrs. Lee?" asked Mrs. Mudge, with new-born politeness. She felt that as a lady of property, Aunt Lucy was entitled to much greater respect and deference than before.

"Thank you, Mrs. Mudge," said Paul, answering for her.

"She won't have occasion for anything in this house. She will get a supply of new things when she gets to New York.

The old lady looked very happy, and Mrs. Mudge, in spite of her outward deference, felt thoroughly provoked at her good fortune.

I will not dwell upon the journey to New York. Aunt Lucy, though somewhat fatigued, bore it much better than she had anticipated. Mr. and Mrs. Cameron entered very heartily into Paul's plans, and readily agreed to receive Aunt Lucy as an inmate of their happy and united household. The old lady felt it to be a happy and blessed change from the Poorhouse, where scanty food and poor accommodations had been made harder to bear by the ill temper of Mr. and Mrs. Mudge, to a home whose atmosphere was peace and kindness.

———

And now, dear reader, it behooves us to draw together the different threads of our story, and bring all to a satisfactory

Mr. and Mrs. Mudge are no longer in charge of the Wrenville Poorhouse. After Aunt Lucy's departure, Mrs. Mudge became so morose and despotic, that her rule became intolerable. Loud complaints came to the ears of 'Squire Newcome, Chairman of the Overseers of the Poor. One fine morning he was compelled to ride over and give the interesting couple warning to leave immediately. Mr. Mudge undertook the charge of a farm, but his habits of intoxication increased upon him to such an extent, that he was found dead one winter night, in a snow-drift, between his own house and the tavern. Mrs. Mudge was not extravagant in her expressions of grief, not having a very strong affection for her husband. At last accounts, she was keeping a boarding-house in a manufacturing town. Some time since, her boarders held an indignation meeting, and threatened to leave in a body unless she improved her fare,—a course to which she was obliged to submit.

George Dawkins, unable to obtain a recommendation from Mr. Danforth, did not succeed in securing another place in New York. He finally prevailed upon his father to advance him a sum of money, with which he went to California. Let us hope that he may "turn over a new leaf" there, and establish a better reputation than he did in New York.

Mr. Stubbs is still in the tin business. He is as happy as the day is long, and so are his wife and children. Once a year he comes to New York and pays Paul a visit. This supplies him with something to talk about for the rest of the year. He is frugal in his expenses, and is able to lay up a couple of hundred dollars every year, which he confides to Paul, in whose financial skill he has the utmost confidence.

I am sure my boy readers would not forgive me for omitting to tell them something more about Ben Newcome. Although his mirthful spirit sometimes led him into mischief, he was good-hearted, and I have known him do many an act of kindness, even at considerable trouble to himself. It will be remembered that in consequence of his night adventure, during which he personated a ghost, much to the terror of Mr. Mudge his father determined to send him to a military school. This proved to be a wise arrangement. The discipline was such as Ben needed, and he soon distinguished himself by his excellence in the military drill. Soon after he graduated, the Rebellion broke out, and Ben was at once, in spite of his youth, elected Captain of the Wrenville company. At the battle of Antiatam he acquitted himself with so much credit that he was promoted to a major. He was again promoted, and when Richmond was evacuated, he was one of the first officers to enter the streets of the Rebel capital, a colonel in command of his regiment. I have heard on high authority, that he is considered one of the best officers in the service.

Mr. and Mrs. Cameron are still living. They are happy in the success and increasing prosperity of Paul, whom they regard as a son. Between them and Aunt Lucy he would stand a very fair chance of being spoiled, if his own good sense and good judgment were not sufficient to save him from such a misfortune. Paul is now admitted to a small interest in the firm, which entitles him to a share in the profits. As Danforth and Co. have done a very extensive business of late years, this interest brings him in a very handsome income. There is only one cause of difference between him and the sexton. He insists that Uncle Hugh, who is getting infirm, should resign his office, as he is abundantly able to support the whole family. But the good sexton loves his duties, and will continue to discharge them as long as he is able.

And now we must bid farewell to Paul. He has battled bravely with the difficulties and discouragements that beset him in early life, he has been faithful to the charge which he voluntarily assumed, and his father's memory is free from reproach. He often wishes that his father could have lived to witness his prosperity? but God has decreed it otherwise. Happy in the love of friends, and in the enjoyment of all that can make life desirable, so far as external circumstances have that power, let us all wish him God speed!

Printed in the United States
785500004B

9 781404 324732